Phoenix

The Boneyard Brotherhood | Book 4

Amber Burns

SCARLET LANTERN
Publishing

Scarlet Lantern Publishing

Chapter 1

Ava

The sun was setting as I rode into town, the warm hues of orange and pink splashed across the sky. I couldn't help but think that maybe, just maybe, this was the fresh start I needed. I was tired of running from my past, my military days haunting me like a ghost that refused to be exorcised. As a former military woman, I had seen my fair share of pain and destruction. I was honorably discharged after serving several tours overseas, but the memories of war still weighed heavy on my soul.

My time in the military had taught me discipline, strength, and resilience, but it had also left me with emotional scars that seemed impossible to heal. I had lost friends on the battlefield, and I couldn't shake the feeling that I should have been able to do more to save them. To make matters worse, my return to civilian life had been far from smooth. I found it difficult to adjust to the mundane routine of everyday life, and I struggled to connect with people who couldn't understand what I had been through.

I parked my bike outside a local bar, deciding to grab a drink before finding a place to stay for the night. As I walked in, I immediately felt the atmosphere shift. The bar was dimly lit and filled with the scent of stale beer and cigarette smoke. I scanned the room, noticing the patrons were mostly rough-looking bikers wearing leather vests adorned with various patches. They all seemed to be part of a club, but their camaraderie made me feel a sense of longing I hadn't expected.

I sat at the bar and ordered a drink, taking in my surroundings. The bartender, a middle-aged woman with a warm smile, started chatting with me. "You're new in town, aren't you?" she asked.

"Yeah, just passing through," I replied, taking a sip of my drink.

"What's your name, sweetheart?" she inquired.

"Ava," I said, offering her a small smile in return.

As I sipped my drink, I couldn't help but overhear the conversation between two men next to me. One was a grizzled, older man with a thick beard and numerous tattoos, while the other was younger, clean-cut, and seemed to be hanging on the older man's every word.

"So, you think we can trust her, Ted?" the younger man asked, his voice laced with skepticism.

The older man, presumably Ted, looked at him and replied, "I don't know yet, but we could use someone with her skills. And she's military, like us. It's worth a shot."

As they continued their conversation, I found myself becoming more and more intrigued. Who were these men, and what kind of club were they a part of? I decided to take a chance and introduce myself, but not just yet. I needed to learn more about this group before I could approach them with confidence.

Over the next hour, I continued to listen in on their conversation, picking up tidbits about their biker club and the sense of brotherhood they shared. I found myself feeling more and more drawn to them, as they seemed to have found a way to channel their past military experiences into something meaningful and supportive.

As I listened in on the conversation between Ted and the younger man, I couldn't help but feel a sense of kinship with them. The sense of brotherhood and camaraderie that they shared was something I had been craving ever since I left the military. I knew I needed to find a way to be a part of it.

I ordered another drink, and as the bartender handed it to me, she nodded in Ted's direction. "You know, they're always looking for good people to join their club. You should go talk to Ted."

Taking her advice, I mustered up the courage to approach Ted. "Excuse me," I said, trying to catch his attention.

Ted looked up from his drink, his eyes narrowing as he assessed me. "What can I do for you?" he asked gruffly.

"I couldn't help but overhear your conversation earlier, and I was wondering if I could ask you a few questions about your club," I said, trying to sound casual.

Ted's gaze lingered on me for a moment before he nodded, seemingly satisfied with my demeanor. "Sure, have a seat."

I slid onto the stool next to him, and the younger man excused himself, leaving us alone. "So, what do you want to know?" Ted asked, taking a swig of his beer.

"Well, first off, what's the name of your club?" I inquired.

"We're the Boneyard Brotherhood," Ted replied. "We're a motorcycle club made up of former military men and women who are looking for a sense of belonging, a purpose, and a way to make a difference."

I nodded, feeling a spark of excitement at the prospect of joining a group that shared my values and experiences. "How do you make a difference?" I asked, genuinely curious.

"We do charity work, raise funds for veterans, and help out in the community," Ted explained. "But we also look out for our own. We have each other's backs, no matter what."

I felt my heart swell with a mixture of hope and longing. "How does someone go about joining the Brotherhood?" I asked, trying to keep my eagerness in check.

Ted studied me for a moment, his eyes searching my face. "Why are you interested in joining us?" he asked.

I hesitated for a moment, unsure of how much to reveal. Finally, I decided to be honest. "I'm a former military, and since I left, I've been struggling to find my place in the world. I miss the sense of purpose and camaraderie I had when I was serving, and from what I've heard, it sounds like the Boneyard Brotherhood could offer me that."

Ted nodded thoughtfully, taking another sip of his beer. "You're right about that. But joining the Brotherhood isn't something we take lightly. We need to be sure that you're someone we can trust, someone who's loyal and committed to our cause."

"I understand," I replied, feeling both nervous and determined. "What do I need to do to prove myself to you?"

Ted leaned back in his chair, his eyes never leaving mine. "First, I need to know more about you. What's your background? What did you do in the military?"

I took a deep breath and began to share my story. I told him about my tours overseas, the friends I had lost, and the emotional scars I carried with me. As I spoke, Ted listened intently, his expression softening with empathy.

When I finished, Ted took a moment to process my story before speaking. "It sounds like you've been through a lot, and I can see why you'd be drawn to the Brotherhood. But we can't just let anyone in. There's a process for becoming a member."

He paused, taking another sip of his beer. "First, you'll need to hang around with us for a while. Get to know the other members, attend our events, and show us that you're serious about wanting to be a part of the club. If the other members vouch for you and think you'd be a good fit, you'll be invited to become a prospect."

"A prospect?" I asked, curious about the term.

Ted nodded. "Yeah, it's a sort of trial period. You'll be expected to follow orders, learn the club's rules, and do whatever tasks are assigned to you. If you can prove yourself during that time, you'll be voted in as a full member."

I thought about his words for a moment, considering the commitment I would be making. I knew that joining the Boneyard Brotherhood would be a significant step, but I couldn't ignore the desire I felt to be a part of something greater than myself, something that could help me heal and find purpose.

"I'm willing to do whatever it takes," I told Ted sincerely.

He studied me for a moment, and then a small smile spread across his face. "Alright, then. I'll introduce you to the others, and we'll see how it goes from there."

As Ted led me over to the group of bikers, I felt a mixture of excitement and apprehension. This was the beginning of a new chapter in my life, one that I hoped would bring me the sense of belonging and purpose I had been searching for.

My heart raced as Ted introduced me to the members of the Boneyard Brotherhood. Each of them eyed me carefully, sizing me up, but there was one man in particular whose gaze seemed to linger on me longer than the others. His name was Alex, and there was something about him that immediately drew me in. His tall, muscular frame, short-cropped dark hair, and piercing blue eyes made it hard for me to look away. I felt a strange sense of familiarity, as if I had known him in a different life, and an undeniable attraction that I couldn't quite comprehend.

As our eyes met, a shiver ran down my spine, and I found myself wondering what kind of man he truly was. Was he as mysterious and intriguing as he appeared to be?

I broke my eye contact with Alex and turned my attention back to Ted, focusing on the task at hand: proving myself to the Boneyard Brotherhood and earning my place among them.

Chapter 2

Alex

I stood in the background as Ted introduced the newest arrival to our clubhouse. Ava was her name, and she was a vision. There was something about her that I couldn't quite put my finger on, but I knew I needed to get to know her. Maybe it was her long, wavy dark hair that seemed to dance around her shoulders, or the confident way she carried herself, showcasing her strength and resilience. Perhaps it was the fact that she was a former military woman just like me, her tattoos a testament to her past. Whatever it was, I couldn't help but be drawn to her.

As the introductions went on, I found my thoughts drifting to Ava. I wondered what her story was, what had brought her to our doorstep. Had she faced the same demons as I had after leaving the military? Did she also search for a sense of belonging and purpose? I knew it was too soon to ask her these questions, but my curiosity was overwhelming.

I couldn't help but notice how Ava's eyes seemed to linger on me for a moment longer than the others. I could feel a connection between us, as if our shared pasts were reaching out and intertwining with one another. It was a strange feeling, one that sent a shiver down my spine and made my heart race.

After the formalities were done, Ted offered Ava a job at the clubhouse. I could see her eyes light up with excitement, but also with a hint of uncertainty. It was obvious that she had been through a lot, and joining our club was a huge step for her. I wanted to assure her that she was making the right choice, to offer her the support she needed, but I knew that it wasn't my place to do so. At least, not yet.

Over the next few days, I found myself seeking out opportunities to talk to Ava, trying to get to know her better. I could tell that she was still adjusting to her new surroundings, and I wanted to make her feel as welcome as possible.

"Hey, Ava," I said one day as I approached her while she was cleaning the bar. "How are you settling in?"

She looked up and smiled, a hint of surprise in her eyes. "Oh, hey, Alex. I'm doing alright, thanks. It's definitely a big change, but I'm getting used to it."

I leaned against the bar, trying to appear casual, but my heart was pounding in my chest. "Yeah, I know what you mean," I replied. "When I first joined the Brotherhood, it was a bit of a shock to the system. But trust me, you'll find your place here soon enough."

Ava looked thoughtful for a moment before asking, "What made you join, if you don't mind me asking?"

I hesitated for a moment, not sure if I was ready to share my own past with her. But there was something about her that made me want to open up, to let her in. "Well," I began, "I used to be in the military, special forces. When I got out, I felt lost. I missed the camaraderie and the sense of belonging. When I found the Boneyard Brotherhood, it was like I found a new family."

Ava's eyes softened as she listened to my story. "I can definitely relate to that feeling," she said quietly. "After leaving the military, it felt like a part of me was missing. It's been difficult finding a place where I fit in since then."

I nodded, understanding all too well what she meant. "It's not easy to leave that life behind," I agreed. "But I think you'll find that the Brotherhood can provide you with the support and the sense of purpose that you've been searching for. We're all in this together, and we've got each other's backs."

Ava smiled, and I could see the appreciation in her eyes. "That's really good to hear, Alex. Thank you for sharing that with me. It makes me feel a bit more at ease about being here."

I returned her smile, feeling a warmth in my chest. "Of course, Ava. If you ever need someone to talk to or have any questions, don't hesitate to reach out. I'm here for you."

She looked genuinely touched by my offer. "I really appreciate that, Alex. It's nice to know that I have someone to turn to in this new environment."

Our conversation continued, with us sharing more about our past experiences and our time in the military. I couldn't help but feel a deep sense of connection with Ava as we talked, and I sensed that she felt it too. There was something powerful in the bond that formed between us, a bond that was forged by our shared experiences and the understanding that only those who had been through similar trials could have.

As our conversation came to an end, I knew that my initial attraction to Ava had grown into something much deeper. I couldn't deny the feelings that were stirring inside me, and I found myself longing to be closer to her, to explore the potential for something more between us. But for now, I knew that we both needed time to adjust to our new roles in the Boneyard Brotherhood and to learn to trust one another fully.

"Thanks for the chat, Alex," Ava said, her eyes filled with warmth and gratitude. "I really needed that."

"You're welcome, Ava," I replied, my heart swelling with emotion. "Just remember that you're not alone here. We're all in this together."

As I walked away, I couldn't help but feel that this was just the beginning of a deep and meaningful relationship between Ava and me. And as I looked back at her, I knew that I would do whatever it took to protect her and to help her find her place in our club. Because that's what the Boneyard Brotherhood was all about – taking care of our own, no matter what.

Chapter 3

Ava

As I stood behind the bar, wiping down the countertop, I couldn't help but feel a sense of belonging within the Boneyard Brotherhood. It was only my first week here, but the warmth and camaraderie I had experienced so far were beyond anything I had expected. The members had welcomed me with open arms, and I was determined to prove myself worthy of their trust and friendship.

I had just finished restocking the shelves when Van Cleef strolled in, his usual charming smile plastered across his face. "Hey, Ava," he said, leaning against the bar. "How's your day going?"

I couldn't help but smile back. "It's going well, thanks. I'm getting the hang of things around here."

"That's great to hear," he replied with a flirtatious wink. "You know, you've already made quite an impression on the guys. Everyone's talking about how lucky we are to have you."

I felt my cheeks warm at the compliment. "I'm the lucky one," I admitted. "I couldn't ask for a better group of people to start this new chapter with."

Van Cleef's eyes sparkled with curiosity. "So, what do you think of the place so far? Is there anything you'd like to change or improve?"

I paused, considering his question. "Well, I love the sense of community and how everyone looks out for one another. As for improvements, maybe we could organize some events to raise funds for local charities or support fellow veterans."

He nodded thoughtfully, his gaze lingering on me for a moment longer than necessary. "That's a great idea, Ava. I'm sure the guys would be up for that. We're always looking for ways to give back to the community and help those in need."

Our conversation shifted to lighter topics, as Van Cleef asked about my favorite hobbies and pastimes. "I love to go for long runs," I told him. "It helps me clear my head and stay focused. Plus, it's a great way to stay in shape."

Van Cleef grinned, his eyes playfully scanning me up and down. "I could definitely use a running partner, especially one as gorgeous as you. How about we go for a run together sometime?"

"That sounds like fun," I agreed, feeling a sense of fellowship forming between us, despite his light flirtations

We continued to chat about everything from our favorite movies to our shared love of motorcycles. It was refreshing to have such an easy-going conversation with someone who understood the challenges I'd faced in the past. It made me feel even more at home in the Boneyard Brotherhood, and I found myself looking forward to getting to know Van Cleef and the other members even better.

As the afternoon wore on, the clubhouse began to fill up with members returning from their various jobs and activities. I busied myself behind the bar, making drinks and serving food, while engaging in light banter with the patrons. It was a far cry from my previous life in the military, but I found a sense of purpose in it, knowing that I was helping to support my new family.

Ted took a seat at the bar and ordered his usual whiskey. "So, Ava," he began, his voice low and gravelly, "how are you settling in?"

I poured him his drink and smiled. "I'm enjoying it more than I thought I would. It's nice to be around people who understand where I've been and what I've been through."

Ted nodded solemnly. "That's what the Brotherhood is all about—looking out for each other and helping one another heal. You're one of us now, and we're here for you, no matter what."

I felt a surge of gratitude and pride as I handed him his whiskey. "Thank you, Ted. That means a lot to me."

Ted took a sip of his drink, looking thoughtful. "You know, when I first started the Brotherhood, I never imagined it would grow into what it is today. It's become a sanctuary for those who need it, a place where we can heal our wounds and find camaraderie."

I leaned against the bar, eager to learn more about the man who had built this community. "What made you start the Brotherhood?"

Ted looked around the room, his eyes taking in the faces of the members who had become his family. "I was lost after my time in the military. I couldn't find a place where I felt like I belonged. The Brotherhood started as just a group of friends, fellow veterans who were struggling to find our way in the world. But over time, it grew into something more. It became a place where we could heal, grow, and find a purpose again."

His words resonated with me, as I was experiencing the same feelings of finding a purpose and a place to belong. "You've created something truly special here, Ted. I'm honored to be a part of it."

Ted raised his glass in a toast. "To the Brotherhood, and to our newest prospect, Ava. Welcome to the family."

As the night went on, I found myself in deep conversations with several members, learning about their lives, their struggles, and their dreams for the future. Wilson, Ted's second in command, shared his plans for expanding the Brotherhood's presence in the community, while Sid, who was a skilled mechanic, lamented about his chronic back pain that made it difficult for him to work on his beloved bikes.

Sid also spoke fondly of Maddie, his girlfriend and a former paralegal, affectionately referring to her as "Sweetcheeks." She had left her old life behind to join the Brotherhood, where she found love and a sense of belonging. Maddie told me about how Sid had helped her through some of her darkest days.

As I listened to their stories, I felt my connection to the Boneyard Brotherhood growing stronger by the minute. It was a tight-knit group that had faced adversity head-on and had come out stronger for it. I knew that I was in the right place, surrounded by people who would stand by me no matter what.

Later that evening, Alex walked in, his piercing blue eyes immediately finding mine. A small smile played on his lips as he approached the bar. "Hey, Ava," he greeted me, his voice warm and inviting. "How's your day been?"

I couldn't help but grin back. The sight of him made my heart race. "It's been great, actually. I've been getting to know everyone better and learning more about the Brotherhood. I feel like I'm really starting to find my place here."

Alex's smile widened. "I'm glad to hear that. I knew you'd fit in perfectly."

I blushed at his words and busied myself with wiping down the counter. "Thanks, Alex. It's been a lot easier with you by my side."

He leaned in closer, his voice lowering to a whisper. "And I wouldn't have it any other way."

Our eyes met, and I felt that familiar spark between us, a burning desire that had been growing stronger ever since we first met. Alex's gaze lingered on my lips for a moment before he pulled back, a playful grin on his face.

"So, tell me, Ava," he said, leaning against the counter, "what's something about you that I don't know yet?"

I raised an eyebrow, considering my response. "Well, I used to play the piano when I was younger. I even won a few competitions. How about you?"

Alex laughed. "Really? I never would've guessed. As for me... I used to be pretty good at drawing, but I haven't picked up a pencil in years."

"Drawing, huh? That's interesting. What did you like to draw?" I asked, genuinely intrigued.

He shrugged. "Mostly people, I guess. I found it fascinating to capture someone's essence on paper."

We continued to exchange small details about our pasts, the conversation flowing easily between us. I told him about my love for action movies and how I had once tried to learn kickboxing, but ended up with a bruised ego and a sprained ankle. Alex admitted that he had a soft spot for romance novels and that he'd even tried his hand at writing one, though he'd never shown it to anyone.

As we talked, the flirting between us intensified. I teased him about his taste in romance novels, asking if he had a favorite trope. He replied with a smirk, saying he had a thing for strong, independent women who could hold their own in a fight.

"Oh, really?" I laughed. "Well, I can't promise you any swoon-worthy declarations of love, but I can definitely hold my own."

"I have no doubt about that," he said, his eyes twinkling with mischief.

However, whenever the subject of his military service came up, Alex became more guarded and vague. I could tell there were parts of his past he wasn't ready to share, but I didn't push him. We all had our secrets.

At one point, Alex playfully teased me about my wavy hair, saying that he couldn't help but imagine running his fingers through it. I countered by telling him how much I admired his strong arms and how safe they made me feel.

The air around us seemed to grow hotter as our words became more daring, but we both knew that the crowded bar was no place for a more intimate encounter. Instead, we continued to talk and laugh, sharing stories and getting to know each other even better.

As the night wore on, I learned about Alex's love for cooking, his favorite books, and how he had a knack for fixing things, from motorcycles to appliances. In turn, I shared my dreams of traveling the world, my fondness for mystery novels, and my guilty pleasure of binge-watching reality TV shows.

Our connection deepened as we discovered more about each other's likes and dislikes, past experiences, and hopes for the future. The conversation felt effortless, as if we'd known each other for years rather than just a few weeks.

As the night came to an end, the clubhouse began to empty, with members heading off to their rooms or leaving for the night. Alex and I remained at the bar, seemingly lost in our conversation and enjoying each other's company.

"I should probably get going," I said reluctantly, glancing at the clock on the wall. "It's getting late, and I have an early start tomorrow."

Alex nodded, though I could tell he was just as reluctant to end our conversation. "Yeah, you're right. Time flies when you're having fun, huh?"

I smiled at him, feeling a warmth in my chest. "It really does. Thank you for tonight, Alex. I had a great time."

He reached out and gently brushed his fingers against my hand, sending shivers down my spine. "The pleasure was all mine, Ava. I'm really glad we got the chance to talk like this."

"Me too," I agreed, my heart pounding in my chest.

We stood up from our stools, and Alex walked me to the door. Our fingers brushed against each other's as we said our goodnights, the tension between us palpable.

"I'll see you tomorrow, Ava," he said softly, his eyes lingering on mine for a moment longer than necessary.

"I'll look forward to it," I replied, my voice barely above a whisper.

With that, we reluctantly parted ways for the night, the memories of our conversation and the undeniable chemistry between us lingering in the air.

As I lay in bed that night, I couldn't help but replay our conversation in my mind. I felt a sense of closeness to Alex that I hadn't experienced with anyone else before. We had only scratched the surface of each other's pasts, but the emotional connection was undeniable.

My thoughts wandered to the possibility of a future with Alex, and I couldn't help but feel a sense of excitement mixed with trepidation. I knew that there were still many obstacles we would need to overcome, including the secrets that he was keeping. But for now, I allowed myself to bask in the warmth of our growing connection.

I tossed and turned in bed, unable to get Alex out of my mind. His rugged handsomeness, the way his eyes seemed to bore into my soul, and the gentle touch of his fingers against my skin left me aching for more. My body felt alive, pulsating with a desire I couldn't deny any longer.

Giving in to my carnal urges, I let my hand trail down my body, my fingers finding the hem of my shirt and slipping beneath it. I caressed my sensitive skin, my thoughts consumed by images of Alex's strong, muscular body pressed against mine. My breathing grew heavy as my fingers found my aching nipple, rolling and pinching it gently.

I moaned softly, imagining Alex's mouth on me, his warm, wet tongue teasing and tasting me. My other hand slid lower, slipping beneath the waistband of my panties. I was soaked with desire, and as my fingers brushed against my swollen clit, a jolt of pleasure shot through me.

As I continued to pleasure myself, I envisioned Alex's skilled hands on my body, his fingers exploring every inch of me. I imagined him pushing me onto the bed, his powerful frame hovering above me as he positioned himself between my legs. His eyes locked onto mine, filled with lust and intensity, making my heart race.

My hips bucked against my hand as I thought of him sliding into me, filling me completely. I envisioned his strong arms supporting his weight, his biceps flexing as he began to thrust into me slowly, deliberately. His breaths would grow heavier, his chiseled chest heaving as our bodies moved together in perfect harmony.

My fingers moved faster, my body tense and quivering with anticipation. I bit my lip to muffle my moans, my thoughts consumed by the fantasy of Alex's body moving in perfect rhythm with mine. As my climax approached, I imagined Alex's lips on mine, our breaths mingling as we shared a passionate, desperate kiss. His fingers would intertwine with mine, pinning my hands above my head as he took control, his thrusts becoming more powerful and urgent.

With a final, shuddering moan, I came, waves of pleasure crashing over me as my body convulsed with ecstasy. As the aftershocks subsided, I lay there, panting and spent.

A sudden wave of embarrassment washed over me, and I quickly pulled my hands away from my body. I couldn't believe I had let my imagination run so wild, indulging in such an intimate fantasy about Alex. But despite the embarrassment, a part of me couldn't help but yearn for the moment when the fantasy might become reality.

I rolled onto my side, pulling the sheets up to my chin and closing my eyes. As sleep finally claimed me, my thoughts were still filled with Alex, our connection, and the passionate possibilities that lay ahead.

Chapter 4

Alex

The sun was just beginning to set as I sat at the bar, watching Ava work with a sense of pride. She had truly become part of the Boneyard Brotherhood, and I couldn't help but admire her strength and determination. As she moved about, laughing and chatting with the other members, I couldn't help but feel a growing sense of attachment to her.

Sid slid onto the barstool beside me, nursing a beer. "You've got it bad, huh?" he remarked with a knowing grin.

I tried to play it off, taking a swig of my own drink. "What are you talking about?"

"Don't play dumb, Alex. You've been watching Ava like a hawk all evening," he said, nudging me with his elbow. "It's pretty obvious you two have something going on."

I couldn't help but smile, feeling a warmth in my chest. "Yeah, I guess you could say that. She's... different from anyone I've ever met."

Sid nodded, taking another sip of his beer. "She's definitely something special. But be careful, man. This life isn't easy, and you've got to be sure she can handle it."

I frowned, knowing he had a point. "I know. I just... I want to protect her, you know?"

Before Sid could respond, the roar of engines approaching the club-house caught our attention. I glanced toward the door, narrowing my eyes as I recognized the emblem on the jackets of the riders – The Night Prowlers, a rival club with a reputation for violence and shady dealings.

"What the hell are they doing here?" Sid muttered, coming up beside me.

I clenched my fists, feeling a surge of anger and protectiveness. "I don't know, but they won't be staying long if I have anything to say about it."

Ted got up from his seat and motioned for me, Wilson, Sid, and a few other members to follow him outside to confront the Night Prowlers. Ava, sensing the danger, had stopped working and was watching us with a mixture of fear and anger.

As we stepped outside, the Night Prowlers dismounted their bikes and swaggered toward us. Ted stepped forward, his expression stern. "What do you want?" he demanded, his voice cold.

Their leader, a tall, broad-shouldered man with a sinister sneer, replied, "We're here to discuss some... business with you."

The air was thick with tension as the two groups faced off. I moved closer, positioning myself between the entrance and the Night Prowlers, my mind on Ava inside the clubhouse.

Suddenly, one of the Night Prowlers lunged at Ted, throwing a punch that connected with his jaw. The sound of the impact sent a shockwave through the crowd, and all hell broke loose.

I sprung into action, my special forces training kicking in as I engaged with the rival club members. My fists flew, each strike calculated and precise. One of them pulled a knife, and I quickly disarmed him, delivering a powerful kick that sent him sprawling to the ground. The adrenaline coursed through my veins, driving me to defend my brothers and Ava.

The fight continued to escalate, the sounds of grunts, punches, and the crack of bones filling the air. I focused on protecting the Boneyard Brotherhood, using every technique I had learned during my time in the special forces. But in the chaos, I felt a sharp pain in my arm and looked down to see a gash from one of the Night Prowlers' knives. The wound was bleeding, but it wasn't deep enough to slow me down.

I continued fighting, ignoring the pain as best I could. When the dust finally settled, the Night Prowlers were beaten and bloodied, retreating to their bikes and fleeing the scene. I looked around, taking stock of the damage and checking on my fellow Boneyard Brotherhood members. We had suffered some injuries, but we were still standing.

As I started to head back inside the clubhouse, Wilson caught my eye and gestured to my injured arm. "You need to get that checked out, man," he said, concern etched on his face.

I nodded, knowing he was right, but my main concern was Ava. "I will, but first I need to make sure Ava is okay."

I hurried back inside the clubhouse, my heart heavy with concern for Ava. I found her sitting on a barstool, her hands shaking as she tried to calm herself. I knew the violence was taking a toll on her, possibly triggering her PTSD from her time in the military.

I approached her slowly, my heart aching. "Ava, are you okay?" I asked gently.

She looked up at me, her green eyes filled with a mix of fear and uncertainty. "I don't know, Alex. I... I didn't expect this. The violence... it's bringing back memories I thought I had buried."

I sat down beside her, wanting nothing more than to comfort and protect her. "I'm sorry, Ava. I never wanted you to have to experience this side of the club. But I promise, I'll do everything I can to keep you safe."

Ava took a deep breath, her hands still trembling. "I know you will, Alex. It's just... I thought I had left this kind of violence behind when I left the military. I don't want it to consume my life again."

I reached out and gently took her hand, feeling the warmth of her skin against mine. "I understand, Ava. And I don't blame you for feeling that way. But the Boneyard Brotherhood is a family, and we protect each other. Sometimes, that means facing violence head-on. But it also means we have each other's backs, no matter what."

She looked into my eyes, searching for reassurance. "I want to believe that, Alex. I really do. But how can I be sure? How can I trust that this life won't drag me back into the darkness?"

I squeezed her hand gently, my heart aching for her pain. "Ava, I won't lie to you – there are no guarantees. But I will do everything in my power to keep you safe and to make sure you never feel like you're alone in this. We're in this together, and I'll be with you every step of the way."

Ava's eyes welled up with tears, and she leaned her head against my shoulder. "Thank you, Alex. I don't know what I would do without you."

I wrapped my arm around her, pulling her close. "You don't ever have to find out. I'm here for you, Ava. And I'm not going anywhere."

We sat there, holding each other as the noise of the clubhouse slowly returned to normal. Despite the chaos that had just occurred, I couldn't help but feel a sense of peace knowing that Ava and I were facing it together.

Chapter 5

Ava

The chaos from the previous night still lingered in the air, but life at the clubhouse was slowly returning to normal. I couldn't shake the feeling of vulnerability, but there was something comforting in knowing that Alex had my back. His strong presence was a beacon of light in the darkness that had threatened to swallow me whole.

As the evening approached, I found myself alone with Alex in a quiet corner of the clubhouse. We sat down, our shoulders touching, the warmth of his body sending shivers down my spine.

"I never really talked about my past before," Alex said softly, his voice barely audible over the distant hum of the clubhouse. "It's not something I like to revisit."

I looked into his deep blue eyes, sensing the pain he was trying to hide. "You don't have to tell me if you don't want to," I assured him, my hand resting gently on his arm. "But sometimes, sharing our demons can help lighten the load."

He hesitated for a moment before taking a deep breath. "I was in the special forces, as you know. I saw things, did things that I'm not proud of. It's hard to shake those memories, even after all these years."

"I understand, Alex," I said, my voice trembling as I remembered my own experiences. "The military changes you, and not always for the better."

He looked at me with a mixture of surprise and understanding. "You know, when I first met you and learned about your military background, I felt a connection with you. It's not often you meet someone who truly understands what you've been through."

"Yeah," I admitted, my eyes downcast. "I served for a few years before I got injured and was discharged. But those memories still haunt me sometimes."

Alex reached over and took my hand, giving it a gentle squeeze. "You're incredibly brave, Ava. To face those demons and still keep going – it's a testament to your strength."

I smiled at his kind words, feeling a warmth spread through me. "Thank you, Alex. That means a lot coming from you."

We fell into a comfortable silence, the weight of our shared pasts forming a bond between us. It was a relief to know that I wasn't alone in my struggles – that Alex understood what I was going through.

After a few moments, Alex spoke again. "You know, when I left the military, I wasn't sure where I was going to end up. But the Boneyard Brotherhood gave me a sense of purpose and belonging that I didn't know I needed."

"I can see that," I agreed, watching the other members of the club going about their business. "It's like a family here, isn't it?"

He nodded, his eyes filled with a mixture of pride and affection. "It is. And it's not just about the bikes and the parties – it's about having each other's backs, no matter what. I'd do anything for these people."

"I feel the same way," I admitted, realizing just how true it was. "I've only been here a short time, but I already feel like I belong."

Alex smiled warmly, his hand still holding mine. "I'm glad to hear that, Ava. And I want you to know that I'll always have your back, too."

The intensity of his gaze made my heart race, and I knew that what was developing between us was more than just a fleeting attraction. It was a deep connection, rooted in our shared experiences and our desire to protect and support each other.

As the night wore on, the laughter and chatter around the clubhouse grew louder, but it felt as if Alex and I were in our own little world. It was a strange yet comforting feeling, knowing that someone else understood the demons that haunted us both.

Eventually, our conversation turned to lighter topics, and we found ourselves laughing and joking like old friends. But every now and then, our eyes would meet, and I could feel the electric charge between us, growing stronger with each passing moment.

Unable to resist the temptation any longer, I leaned in closer to Alex, my lips hovering mere inches from his. "Alex," I whispered, my breath warm against his skin. "I can't stop thinking about you."

His eyes searched mine, filled with an intense desire that mirrored my own. "Ava," he murmured, his voice thick with emotion. "I feel the same way."

With that, our lips met in a searing kiss that sent a shockwave of passion through my entire body. I could feel Alex's strong arms wrap around me, pulling me closer to him as our tongues danced together in a sensual tango.

As our kiss deepened, Alex guided me towards a dimly lit backroom of the clubhouse, the sounds of the party fading into the background. Once inside, he gently pushed me up against the wall, his hands roaming over my body, igniting a fire within me that I had never experienced before.

My hands moved to the hem of his shirt, desperately trying to rid him of the barrier between us. Alex responded eagerly, lifting his arms to allow me to pull the fabric over his head. I couldn't help but admire his muscular chest, the result of years of military training and discipline.

Alex's hands moved to the buttons of my blouse, skillfully undoing each one as his lips continued to devour mine. As the last button was undone, my blouse fell open, revealing my lace bra. Alex's eyes roamed over me, taking in every inch of my exposed skin.

"You're so beautiful, Ava," he whispered, his voice filled with wonder.

I blushed at his compliment, feeling a thrill of excitement run through me. My fingers fumbled with the buckle of his belt, eager to explore the body that had haunted my dreams for weeks. Once I had successfully undone his belt and jeans, I pushed them down, along with his boxer briefs, allowing them to pool at his feet.

Standing there, exposed to one another, I couldn't help but feel vulnerable. But as I looked into Alex's eyes, I saw nothing but admiration and desire, which helped ease my insecurities. His hands reached out, gently cupping my face as he pressed another tender kiss to my lips.

"You're sure about this, Ava?" he asked, his voice laced with concern. "I don't want to push you into anything."

I smiled at his consideration, my heart swelling with affection for this man. "I've never been more sure about anything in my life," I whispered, my eyes locked onto his.

A slow grin spread across his face, and he leaned in to capture my lips once more, his hands trailing down my body until they reached the waistband of my jeans. He deftly unbuttoned and unzipped them, slipping his fingers beneath the fabric to slide them down my legs. As I stepped out of them, I was left in just my bra and panties, my body shivering with anticipation.

Alex's gaze never left mine as he reached behind me, expertly unclasping my bra and allowing it to fall to the floor. My breath hitched as his strong hands moved to my hips, his fingers hooking beneath the edges of my panties and slowly lowering them down my legs. The feeling of being completely bare before him was both exhilarating and terrifying.

"God, Ava," he breathed, drinking in the sight of me. "You have no idea how much I've wanted this."

"Show me," I urged him, my voice thick with desire. "Show me how much you want me, Alex."

His eyes darkened with lust, and he pressed me against the wall once more, his lips hungrily exploring my neck and collarbone. I moaned in pleasure as his mouth found my breast, his tongue teasing and tantalizing my sensitive nipple. My hands gripped his shoulders, my fingers digging into his muscles as waves of pleasure coursed through me.

As he continued to lavish attention on my breasts, his hand drifted lower, his fingers slipping between my thighs. I gasped at the intimate touch, my body arching into his as he gently stroked my most sensitive areas.

"Alex," I whimpered, my body trembling with need. "Please..."

He seemed to understand my unspoken plea, and his fingers moved to part my slick folds, his thumb brushing against my clit in a way that made my knees go weak. My breath came in short gasps as he continued to tease and touch me, driving me closer and closer to the edge.

"I need you, Ava," he whispered against my skin. "I need to be inside you."

"Please," I begged, my voice barely more than a breathless moan. "I need you too."

With a nod, he stepped back just enough to give himself room to maneuver. He lifted one of my legs, wrapping it around his waist, and guided himself to my entrance. Our eyes locked as he slowly pushed inside me, filling me in a way that made my body sing with pleasure.

The sensation of him filling me completely left me breathless, and I could see the same effect in his eyes. We held each other's gaze as he began to move, his hips rocking gently at first, allowing me to adjust to him. The pleasure was already building within me, and I couldn't help but moan his name as he picked up the pace, each thrust driving us closer and closer to the edge.

Our lips met in a searing kiss, our tongues dancing together as our bodies moved in perfect harmony. I could feel the tension building within me, each stroke of his cock bringing me closer to that sweet release I craved. My hands moved to his hair, tugging on the dark strands as I urged him on.

"Alex," I whispered against his lips. "I'm so close..."

His hand slipped between us, his fingers once again finding my clit and teasing it with expert precision. The added stimulation was all I needed, and I felt my orgasm wash over me like a tidal wave, my body clenching around him as I cried out in ecstasy.

The sight of me coming undone beneath him seemed to be Alex's undoing as well. He buried his face in the crook of my neck, his breath hot against my skin as he moaned my name, his thrusts becoming more erratic as he neared his own climax. With one final, deep stroke, he stilled, his body shuddering with pleasure as he released inside of me.

For a moment, we stayed like that, our bodies pressed together, our breaths mingling as we came down from the intense high of our lovemaking. Alex's arms wrapped around me, holding me close as our heart rates slowly returned to normal.

"You're incredible," he murmured, placing a soft kiss on my temple. "I can't even begin to describe how amazing that was."

I smiled, feeling a warmth spread through me at his words. "It was incredible for me too, Alex. I never imagined that being with you could feel this... perfect."

As we stood there, basking in the afterglow of our passion, I realized that despite the chaos and danger that surrounded us, I had found a sense of belonging in the Boneyard Brotherhood – and in Alex's arms. And for the first time in a long time, I felt truly content.

We eventually cleaned up and got dressed, our fingers intertwined as we made our way back to the main room of the clubhouse. The knowledge of the intimate connection we had just shared only strengthened my resolve to stand by the Boneyard Brotherhood and Alex, no matter what challenges we faced together.

Chapter 6

Ava

As the days went by, I found myself becoming more and more entrenched in the Boneyard Brotherhood's world. I spent time with the various members, learning about the club's operations, goals, and the sense of camaraderie that bound them together. They were a family, and I couldn't help but feel a sense of belonging that I had been missing for so long.

One day, as I was helping Cindy in the kitchen, she started to open up about her life in the club. "You know, Ava, when I first joined the Brotherhood, I was a bit skeptical," she admitted, her eyes distant as she chopped vegetables. "I thought it was just going to be a wild party all the time, but it turned out to be so much more than that."

I looked at her curiously, urging her to continue. "What do you mean?"

Cindy smiled, her eyes meeting mine. "Well, for starters, everyone here genuinely cares about each other. We're not just friends – we're family. And not only do we have each other's backs, but we also help our community. We support local businesses, organize charity events, and work together to make life better for those around us."

I nodded, understanding that beneath their rough exteriors, the members of the Boneyard Brotherhood had hearts of gold. "That sounds amazing, Cindy. I'm really starting to see what you mean."

She grinned, giving me a knowing look. "Just give it some time, Ava. You'll come to see that this club is more than just leather jackets and motorcycles."

After finishing up in the kitchen, I made my way to the bar where Ted was nursing a beer. He looked up as I approached, a serious expression on his face. "Ava, have a seat. I wanted to talk to you about the club's mission."

I sat down beside him, eager to learn more. "What's on your mind, Ted?"

"We're not just a bunch of outlaws, Ava," he told me earnestly, his eyes filled with conviction. "We help our community, support local business-es, and work together to make life better for those around us. Sure, we may have our share of enemies, like the Night Prowlers, but we're a force for good."

I listened intently as Ted shared stories about the club's various phil-anthropic efforts and community outreach programs. It was clear that he was deeply committed to making a positive impact in the world, and I felt a surge of pride at the thought of being associated with such a group.

"So, what do you think, Ava?" Ted asked, his gaze searching my face for any hint of hesitation. "Do you think you can get behind what we stand for?"

I thought about it for a moment before responding, my voice firm and filled with conviction. "Absolutely, Ted. I've seen firsthand how much you all care about each other and the people in this community. I'm proud to be a part of the Boneyard Brotherhood."

Ted smiled, clapping me on the back. "That's what I like to hear. Welcome to the family, Ava."

I couldn't help but grin back, feeling a sense of belonging that I hadn't felt in a long time.

As the weeks went by, the Night Prowlers were relentless in their harassment. They'd leave threatening messages scrawled on the walls of our clubhouse, damage our bikes, and even followed some of our members when they were out on runs. It was clear that they were trying to intimidate us, but we refused to back down.

Ted had called a meeting to discuss how we could best protect ourselves and our community from the Night Prowlers' aggression. We brainstormed ideas, from setting up surveillance cameras to organizing extra patrols. Everyone was committed to ensuring the safety of the Boneyard Brotherhood and the people we served.

After the meeting, Alex and I decided to spend the evening together at the clubhouse. We needed a break from the stress of the situation, and it was the perfect opportunity to unwind and relax in each other's company.

We started the evening playing pool, laughing and teasing each other as we took turns taking shots. Alex's strong arms wrapped around me as he showed me how to hold the cue properly, and I couldn't help but shiver at his touch. His warm breath tickled my ear as he whispered tips and words of encouragement, sending shivers down my spine.

Later, we moved over to the bar, where we shared a few drinks and deep conversation. As we talked about the ongoing situation with the Night Prowlers, Cole and Chase joined us, their expressions serious.

"I'm worried about you two," I admitted, taking a sip of my drink. "You've been really on edge lately, and I can't help but think that this whole thing is taking a toll on you both."

Cole sighed, rubbing his temples. "Yeah, it's been tough. We're doing our best to keep everyone safe, but these bastards are relentless. It's like they're always one step ahead of us."

Chase chimed in, his voice tense. "It's true. We've been working non-stop trying to figure out their next move, but it's like chasing shadows. It's frustrating as hell."

Alex nodded, his expression serious. "We need to come up with a solid plan to put an end to this before it gets any worse. I don't want to see anyone get hurt."

We spent the next couple of hours discussing possible strategies and sharing our concerns about the club's safety. Ideas were thrown around, from increasing our patrols to trying to gather more intel on the Night Prowlers.

"I think we should consider reaching out to some of our contacts in law enforcement," Chase suggested. "Maybe they can help us find a way to deal with these guys before things escalate any further."

Cole nodded in agreement. "It's worth a shot. We can't keep going on like this, constantly looking over our shoulders. It's not good for the club, and it's not good for the community we're trying to protect."

Alex leaned forward, his brow furrowed. "What about trying to infiltrate their ranks? If we can get someone on the inside, we might be able to figure out their motives and put a stop to this."

Chase considered the idea, his eyes narrowing. "It's risky, but it might be our best shot. If we can find someone they trust, someone who can blend in without raising suspicions, we might be able to gather the intel we need."

Cole took a swig of his drink, grimacing. "But who would we send? We can't risk exposing one of our own to those scumbags."

We continued debating the pros and cons of each idea, trying to find the most effective approach to dealing with the Night Prowlers. It was clear that there was no perfect solution, and each option came with its own risks and uncertainties.

As the night wore on, our conversation began to take on a more somber tone. The weight of the situation settled heavily on our shoulders, and it was evident that the stress was taking a toll on all of us. Despite our determination to protect the Boneyard Brotherhood and the community, the seemingly endless battle against the Night Prowlers was exhausting.

Ava finally broke the silence, her voice soft but firm. "I know it's hard, and I know we're all feeling the pressure. But we can't let the Night Prowlers win. We've all faced adversity before, and we've always come out on top. We'll figure this out, together."

Alex reached across the table to grasp my hand, giving it a reassuring squeeze. "Ava's right. We're a family, and we'll do whatever it takes to keep each other safe. We just need to stay united and focused."

Cole and Chase nodded, their expressions resolute. "We've got your back, no matter what," Cole affirmed, his gaze unwavering. "We'll find a way to put an end to this. Together."

With renewed determination, we continued to discuss potential strategies late into the night. Although the path ahead was uncertain, and the challenges we faced were daunting, the unbreakable bond between the members of the Boneyard Brotherhood gave us the strength and hope we needed to face whatever lay ahead.

As the evening wound down and our conversation gradually shifted to lighter topics, we all shared a deep sense of camaraderie and unity. Though the Night Prowlers continued to threaten our safety and well-being, we knew that we could rely on each other to face any challenge.

In the quiet moments between discussions, I found myself stealing glances at Alex, who seemed to be doing the same. Our eyes met, and a silent understanding passed between us. Amidst the chaos and uncertainty, we had found solace and strength in each other's arms. And as we faced the trials that lay ahead, we knew that our love would be our greatest weapon in the fight against the Night Prowlers.

Chapter 7

Alex

As I watched Ava from across the room, her laughter filling the air, I couldn't help but smile. She had become such an important part of my life in such a short amount of time, and I found myself drawn to her every moment we spent together.

I walked over to her, and as she looked up at me, her green eyes seemed to sparkle. "Hey, gorgeous," I teased, "I was thinking, since we're both off duty, how about we go for a ride? Just the two of us?"

Ava's face lit up at the suggestion, and she playfully tilted her head. "Oh, really? Are you asking me out on a date, Alex?" she asked with a grin.

I chuckled and scratched the back of my head. "Well, I wouldn't exactly call it a date, but if it makes you happy to think of it that way, then sure," I replied, giving her a wink.

She laughed and playfully nudged my shoulder. "Alright, you got yourself a date. Let's go."

We geared up, grabbing our helmets and jackets, and headed out to the parking lot where our motorcycles were parked. As I straddled my sleek black bike, I looked over at Ava, who had already mounted her own motorcycle. The excitement in her eyes was unmistakable, and I couldn't help but grin in response.

We set off, the wind whipping past us as we navigated the winding roads. The sun was beginning to set, casting a warm, golden light on the landscape as we rode side by side. It was one of those perfect moments, where the rest of the world seemed to fade away, leaving only the two of us and the open road.

As we continued our ride, I spotted a small, hidden path that led off the main road and into the woods. Intrigued, I glanced over at Ava and signaled for her to follow me. We veered off onto the path, the trees closing in around us as we ventured deeper into the woods.

Eventually, we came across a beautiful clearing bathed in the warm glow of the setting sun. The grass was soft and inviting, and I couldn't help but think it was the perfect spot for us to take a break and enjoy each other's company. I slowed my bike to a stop, and Ava did the same, her eyes taking in the serene surroundings.

"Wow, Alex," she said, her voice filled with awe. "This place is incredible. How did you find it?"

I chuckled, removing my helmet and running a hand through my hair. "Honestly, I didn't know it was here. But I'm glad we found it."

We dismounted our bikes and walked towards the center of the clearing, the tall grass whispering around our legs. Ava turned to face me, her green eyes glistening with warmth as she reached out and gently touched my arm.

"Thank you for finding this, for bringing me here," she said softly, and I could see the gratitude in her eyes.

I smiled and reached up to gently tuck a strand of her wavy dark hair behind her ear. "You're welcome, Ava. I couldn't think of anyone else I'd rather share this moment with."

The tenderness in her gaze deepened, and she leaned in to close the distance between us. Our lips met, the kiss slow and gentle at first but growing in intensity as our passion took over. Our hands roamed each other's bodies, the sensation of her curves beneath my fingertips driving me wild. I could feel the heat radiating from her, and I knew she felt it too.

As we broke away for air, Ava looked into my eyes, her breathing heavy. "Alex," she whispered, "I want you."

Her words sent a shiver down my spine, and my desire for her intensified. "Are you sure, Ava?" I asked, wanting to be certain that this was what she truly wanted.

She nodded, her eyes locked onto mine. "I've never been more sure of anything in my life."

I couldn't resist her any longer. We carefully lowered ourselves onto the soft grass, our bodies pressed together as we continued to explore each other with our hands and lips. Our clothing soon became an unwelcome barrier, and we shed them without hesitation, desperate to feel the fullness of each other's touch.

As I continued to kiss my way down her body, I paused to admire the beauty of her navel, playfully dipping my tongue into it before continuing my journey. I could feel the tension building in her body, her desire for me evident in her every breath and movement. Her skin was flushed, the heat radiating off her like a beacon, and I was drawn to it, my hands and mouth eager to explore every inch of her.

I caressed the smooth skin of her inner thighs, my fingers teasingly close to her core, and her hips bucked slightly in response. I grinned, feeling a sense of satisfaction at being able to elicit such reactions from her. I took my time, slowly trailing my fingers up and down her thighs, teasing her until she was practically writhing beneath me.

Finally, I returned my attention to her breasts, the fullness of them fitting perfectly in my hands as I gently squeezed and massaged them.

I took turns lavishing each nipple with my mouth, alternating between sucking, nibbling, and gently flicking my tongue across the sensitive nubs. Ava's moans grew louder, her fingers tightening in my hair as she pulled me closer, urging me to continue.

As I reached her core, I paused, looking up at her and seeing the desire written plainly on her face. I blew a gentle stream of air over her sensitive folds, watching as her body shuddered in response, before pressing my lips to her with a soft, tender kiss. I traced the outline of her with my tongue, exploring her slowly and deliberately, savoring the taste of her arousal.

With each lick, I could feel her body tensing, the muscles in her thighs quivering as she grew closer to the edge. I pressed my tongue flat against her, increasing the pressure, and her hips bucked off the ground, a strangled moan escaping her lips. Encouraged by her response, I focused my attention on her clit, swirling my tongue around it before gently sucking it into my mouth.

Ava's moans became more urgent, her hips undulating as she sought to increase the friction between us. Sensing her impending release, I slid a finger inside her, curving it to reach that sensitive spot deep within her. The combination of my finger and tongue sent her spiraling over the edge, her body convulsing in a powerful orgasm that left her breathless and spent.

As she lay there, trying to catch her breath, I took a moment to admire the way the sunlight filtered through the trees, casting a golden glow on her skin. I couldn't help but think that she looked like a goddess, a vision of beauty and strength that left me in awe.

Feeling a renewed sense of desire, I positioned myself between her legs, the head of my erection teasing her entrance. I met her eyes, seeking her consent, and she gave me a slow, sultry smile, wrapping her legs around my waist and pulling me closer. I slowly pushed into her, savoring the sensation of her warmth enveloping me, and we both let out a deep, guttural groan.

Our bodies moved in perfect harmony, our pace slow and sensual, as we reveled in the connection we shared. With every thrust, I could feel our bond deepening, the trust and understanding between us growing stronger. Our bodies were slick with sweat, the sounds of our passion echoing through the clearing as we surrendered to our desires.

As our rhythm began to quicken, I reached between us to circle her clit with my thumb, wanting to bring her even more pleasure. Ava's nails dug into my back, her legs tightening around me as her moans grew louder and more urgent. The sight of her pleasure, the feeling of her body gripping me so tightly, was intoxicating, driving me closer to the edge with each passing moment.

Ava's eyes locked onto mine, and I could see the love and trust shining brightly within them. It was in that moment that I realized just how deeply I cared for her, how much she meant to me. My heart swelled with emotion, and I knew that I would do anything to protect her, to keep her safe and happy.

Our bodies continued to move together, the intensity of our passion building like a raging storm. I could feel the familiar tightening in my abdomen, signaling my impending release, but I was determined to bring Ava to the heights of pleasure once more before I allowed myself to succumb to my own desires.

As I continued to thrust into her, I increased the pressure on her clit, determined to bring her with me. Ava's breathing grew ragged, her moans turning to high-pitched cries as her body tensed, preparing for the final climax. The sight of her in such a state of ecstasy was enough to push me over the edge, and with a final, powerful thrust, we both tumbled into the abyss of pleasure together.

Our orgasms rocked our bodies, leaving us both panting and trembling in the aftermath. I collapsed on top of her, our bodies slick with sweat and tangled together like the roots of the trees surrounding us. We lay there for a few moments, our breathing slowly returning to normal, as we basked in the afterglow of our passion.

I gently pulled out of her, rolling onto my side and pulling Ava close to me. We lay there in the clearing, the sunlight dappling our skin through the leaves overhead, and I knew that we had found something special together. Our shared experiences, our pasts, had brought us together, but it was our love for one another that would carry us forward.

As we lay there in the clearing, the sun slowly beginning its descent behind the trees, I knew that this was the perfect time to share my past with Ava. We had connected so deeply, and I felt that it was important for her to understand where I came from, the experiences that had shaped me into the man I was today.

"Ava," I began, my voice soft and hesitant, "there's something I want to share with you. About my past, my time in the special forces." I could feel her body tense slightly against mine, but she looked at me with those gorgeous green eyes, filled with love and understanding.

"Alex, you know you can tell me anything," she replied, her voice gentle and encouraging.

Taking a deep breath, I started telling her about my time in the special forces. "I joined the special forces after a few years in the military. I wanted to challenge myself, to be the best I could be, and I knew that the special forces would push me to my limits."

"What was the training like?" Ava asked, her curiosity piqued.

"It was the hardest thing I've ever done," I admitted. "Physically and mentally exhausting. We trained in all types of environments, from the desert to the mountains, learning advanced combat and survival techniques."

Ava nodded, her eyes filled with understanding. "I can only imagine what you went through. I remember my own basic training, and that was tough enough."

I smiled at her, grateful for her empathy. "It wasn't just the physical challenges, though. The mental aspect was just as important. We had to learn to think quickly, to make life-and-death decisions under extreme pressure."

She reached out to touch my hand, her fingers tracing the lines of my palm. "That must have been so difficult, Alex. The weight of those decisions, the lives you were responsible for..."

"Yeah," I sighed, remembering some of the darker moments from my past. "There were times when I questioned if I'd made the right choice, if I could live with the consequences of my actions. But the bonds I formed with my brothers in arms, the sense of purpose and camaraderie, it helped me get through those tough times."

Ava looked at me with such tenderness and love, and I could see the admiration in her eyes. "Alex, I can't even begin to understand everything you've been through, but I can see the incredible strength and resilience you've gained from your experiences. And it's clear how much you care about the people you served with."

I nodded, feeling a surge of gratitude for her understanding. "Thank you, Ava. It means so much to me that you can see that. And now, being part of the Boneyard Brotherhood, I've found a new sense of purpose, a new family."

Ava smiled softly. "I'm so glad you've found that, Alex. And I'm grateful to be a part of it, too. Our shared experiences, our time in the military, it's brought us together in a way I never expected."

I pulled her closer, wrapping my arms around her and burying my face in her soft hair. "Ava, you've given me something I never thought I'd have again – a reason to trust, a reason to hope. Our shared experiences have brought us together, and I know that together we can face anything."

As we lay there, our bodies entwined, I knew that our bond had been strengthened by our shared pasts, by our understanding of each other's struggles and triumphs. We had found solace and love in each other, and I was more certain than ever that we were meant to be together, to face the challenges of life side by

Chapter 8

Ava

It had been a long day, and all I wanted was to share a few drinks with Alex at the clubhouse. I hoped it would help us unwind and take our minds off the challenges we had been facing lately. As we entered the dimly lit room, I could sense the atmosphere was different – something was off. I glanced at Alex, and he seemed to feel it too.

We made our way to the bar, where we found Van Cleef nursing a beer. "Hey, you two," he greeted us with a half-hearted smile. "You might want to grab a drink. We've got a situation."

I raised an eyebrow, curiosity piqued. "What's going on?"

Van Cleef sighed, taking a swig of his beer before answering. "The Night Prowlers proposed a truce. But there's a catch – they want our help with a heist."

Alex's grip on my hand tightened, and I could feel the tension radiating from him. I took a deep breath, trying to steady my nerves. This was unexpected and could potentially put the Boneyard Brotherhood in a precarious position.

As we sat down with our drinks, the rest of the club members began to file into the clubhouse, discussing the Night Prowlers' proposal. Opinions were divided, and the room buzzed with tension as the members argued about whether or not we should accept the offer.

Sid grumbled, "I don't trust them one bit. This is probably some sort of trap."

Maddie, his wife, countered, "But if there's a chance for peace, shouldn't we at least consider it?"

Cole chimed in, his voice stern, "We need to think this through carefully. We can't just jump into something like this without considering the consequences."

Dylan, Cole's partner, added, "We've all lost too much in this war already. If there's a chance to end it, we need to at least hear them out."

The back-and-forth continued, with Alex and I mostly staying quiet, trying to process the situation. I could tell that this decision was weighing heavily on Alex, and I knew it would test our relationship. Would our bond be strong enough to withstand this challenge?

Chase, leaned forward, his expression serious. "Look, I know we don't trust the Night Prowlers, but we can't afford to let our guard down. We need to think strategically here."

Tara, Chase's girlfriend, nodded in agreement. "We have to be smart about this. If we're going to consider their proposal, we need to have a plan in place to protect ourselves."

We locked eyes, and Alex reached out to squeeze my hand. "Ava, what do you think?" he asked in a low voice, seeking my opinion.

I hesitated before answering, my voice wavering, "I... I don't know, Alex. I'm scared. What if this is a trap, and we're just walking right into it?"

Alex nodded, his eyes filled with a mix of concern and determination. "I understand your fears, Ava. But I can't help but think about the possibility of putting an end to this violence. I worry about your safety, and I can't bear the thought of losing you."

Ted finally spoke up, his voice commanding the room's attention. "Alright, everyone. We've all made our points. Let's sleep on it, and we'll reconvene tomorrow to make a decision."

After the meeting adjourned, Alex and I found a quiet corner of the clubhouse to continue our discussion.

"Ava, I know you're scared," Alex said, his blue eyes filled with concern. "I am too. But if we can help put an end to this violence, isn't it worth considering?"

I bit my lip, struggling to find the right words. "I understand where you're coming from, Alex. I really do. But the Night Prowlers have given us no reason to trust them. We could be walking into a trap, and I don't want to risk losing you or anyone else in the club."

Alex ran a hand through his short-cropped hair, frustration evident on his face. "I know, Ava. I know. But if we don't at least try to find a solution, the violence will never end. And the thought of you being in danger because of this ongoing conflict... it terrifies me."

We spent the rest of the night discussing the pros and cons of the heist, our voices barely audible above the distant hum of the clubhouse. Neither of us could find a clear solution, and as we finally fell asleep in each other's arms, the decision still loomed over us.

The next morning, the sun was barely peeking over the horizon as the members of the Boneyard Brotherhood gathered once again to discuss the Night Prowlers' proposal. I sat next to Alex, gripping his hand tightly, my heart pounding in my chest.

Ted cleared his throat, commanding the room's attention once more. "Alright, everyone. We've had a night to think about it. It's time to make a decision. What do we do about the Night Prowlers' offer?"

The room erupted in a cacophony of voices as the members began to voice their opinions. Some were in favor of considering the truce, while others vehemently opposed it, still distrusting the Night Prowlers' intentions.

Wilson offered his opinion. "I think we should consider their offer, but we need to be cautious. We can't afford to let our guard down."

Van Cleef nodded in agreement. "We should listen to what they have to say, but always be prepared for anything. Trust is earned, not given."

Cindy chimed in from the back of the room, her voice trembling slightly. "I'm worried about what could happen, but if there's a chance for peace, I think we should take it."

Cole grumbled as he crossed his arms. "I don't like it, but if it'll put an end to the bloodshed, I'll go along with it. But we better be damn careful."

Sid glanced at Maddie before speaking up. "I don't trust those Night Prowlers, but if we can find a way to ensure our safety and stop this senseless fighting, it might be worth the risk."

The debate went on for quite some time, with members sharing their concerns and discussing the potential consequences of their decision. Alex spoke up, his voice steady and resolute. "We can't keep living in fear. If there's a chance to end this war and protect our loved ones, we owe it to ourselves and to our brothers and sisters to take it."

As the conversation continued, it became apparent that the majority of the club members were leaning towards accepting the Night Prowlers' proposal, despite their hesitations. I looked around the room, taking in the faces of those I had come to consider family. The decision to go through with the heist wasn't an easy one, but it seemed as though it was the only option left to us.

Finally, Ted raised his hand, silencing the room. "Alright, it's clear we're all on the same page here. We'll go through with the heist, but we'll do it on our terms. We'll be cautious, and we'll be prepared for anything. The safety of our family comes first."

A murmur of agreement spread throughout the room, and despite the uncertainty that lay ahead, a sense of unity filled the air. We would face this challenge together, as a brotherhood.

As the clock ticked closer to the start of my shift at the bar, the club members began to disperse, their minds set on the daunting task ahead. The path ahead was uncertain, but together, we would face whatever challenges awaited us.

Chapter 9

Ava

As the Boneyard Brotherhood reluctantly agreed to help the Night Prowlers for the sake of peace, I found myself needing a moment away from the chaos. I decided to speak with Maddie, Dylan, and Tara. We found a quiet corner in the clubhouse, and I opened up about the uneasy truce between the rival clubs.

"I can't believe we're going along with this," I said, my voice heavy with concern. "The Night Prowlers are ruthless. I can't help but feel like we're walking into a trap."

Maddie placed a comforting hand on my shoulder. "I know it's scary, Ava, but we've got to trust in our brothers and sisters. We're all in this together. Besides, Ted and the others wouldn't have agreed to it if they didn't think it was the best option."

Dylan chimed in, her no-nonsense demeanor showing through. "Ava, we'll be cautious and prepared for anything. We have to give it a chance if it means putting an end to this bloodshed. And you know as well as anyone that the Boneyard Brotherhood can handle themselves in tough situations."

Tara, ever the voice of reason, added, "Besides, we've got your back, and you know Alex will do everything in his power to protect you and the club."

"You're right," I sighed, trying to find solace in their words. "I just can't shake this feeling of unease. I hope I'm wrong."

Maddie gave me a reassuring smile. "We all have our reservations, but sometimes, we have to take risks for the greater good. It's part of being in the Boneyard Brotherhood."

As we talked, I found myself growing closer to Maddie, Dylan, and Tara, grateful for their friendship and support. They listened to my concerns and offered their own insights, helping me navigate the complex emotions that came with being part of the Boneyard Brotherhood.

"So, how's it going with you and Alex?" Maddie asked, a teasing smile on her face.

At the mention of Alex's name, my cheeks flushed slightly, and the conversation shifted gears. The other women exchanged knowing glances, clearly eager to discuss my budding relationship with him.

I hesitated for a moment before admitting, "It's incredible. I never thought I'd feel this way about anyone, especially not after everything I've been through. But he's so different from anyone else I've ever known."

Dylan nodded, a knowing smile on her lips. "He's a good man, Ava. You two deserve each other. And it's great to see both of you so happy."

Tara leaned in, her eyes sparkling with curiosity. "So, have you two, you know, taken things to the next level?"

I bit my lip, hesitating before responding, "Yes, we have. And it's been... amazing."

Maddie grinned, clearly excited for me. "That's fantastic, Ava! We're all so happy for you. And it's about time you had some happiness in your life."

Dylan agreed, her expression softening. "Just remember, Ava, we're here for you. If you ever need to talk or vent, don't hesitate to reach out to us."

"Thanks, guys," I said, feeling genuinely touched by their support.

Tara then decided to share some of her own experiences. "Chase and I had a rough start, you know, with our jobs and everything. But we made it work. Love can overcome a lot of obstacles, and it seems like you and Alex are proof of that."

Maddie chimed in, "Sid and I had our fair share of challenges too, but we pushed through them. Communication is key, Ava. Just remember to always be honest with Alex about your feelings, and I'm sure you two will be just fine."

As our conversation continued, we shared more personal stories and advice about our relationships. The bond between the women of the Boneyard Brotherhood only grew stronger, and I felt grateful to be surrounded by such caring and understanding friends.

Later that evening, Alex invited me over to his apartment for dinner. The warm glow of the candlelight and the delicious aroma of the home-cooked meal he'd prepared made me feel at ease despite my lingering concerns about the alliance with the Night Prowlers.

As we sat down to eat, I decided to share my worries with Alex. "I'm still not sure about this whole truce thing, Alex. It just feels so...dangerous."

He nodded, his blue eyes filled with understanding. "I know, Ava. I have my reservations too. But I trust in Ted's judgment, and I believe that we can handle whatever comes our way."

I sighed, looking down at my plate. "I trust you, Alex. I just can't help but be afraid."

Alex reached across the table, taking my hand in his. "I'll do everything in my power to protect you and the club, Ava. You know that."

"I do," I whispered, meeting his gaze. "Thank you, Alex."

As the evening wore on, our conversation turned to lighter topics, and I found myself falling even more deeply in love with Alex. His laughter, his smile, and the way he looked at me all made me feel cherished and valued in a way I never thought possible.

After dinner, we retreated to the living room, where Alex pulled me into his arms. As he kissed me, I felt my worries about the Night Prowlers and the truce fading away. In that moment, all that mattered was the connection between us.

Our passion grew, and we found ourselves tangled together on the couch, exploring one another's bodies with eager hands and hungry mouths. As Alex traced kisses down my neck, I felt a shiver of anticipation run down my spine. The passion between us was electric, and I couldn't help but lose myself in the intensity of our connection.

As our kisses grew deeper and more passionate, I felt a sudden urge to explore Alex's body in a more intimate way. I moved my hands to his waist, gently pushing him back onto the couch. His eyes locked onto mine, filled with a mixture of surprise and desire.

Slowly, I trailed kisses down his chest and abdomen, pausing to tease his skin with my tongue. I could feel his muscles tense beneath my touch, and the sound of his low groans spurred me on. My hands brushed against the waistband of his boxers, and I could feel his hardened length beneath the fabric.

I looked up at him, our eyes connecting as I hooked my fingers into the waistband and slid his boxers down his legs, revealing his arousal. The sight of him made my heart race, and my desire for him intensified. I placed a tender kiss on the tip of his length, tasting the hint of saltiness as his breath hitched in response.

With my hand wrapped firmly around the base, I took him into my mouth, inch by slow inch. I could feel the heat of him on my tongue, and the weight of him as I took him deeper. Alex's fingers tangled in my hair, his grip tightening as I began to move my head in a slow rhythm.

I glanced up at him, and the sight of his flushed face and the lust in his eyes sent a thrill through me. I focused on the task at hand, swirling my tongue around him, applying gentle suction as I took him in deeper. Alex's groans grew louder, and his grip in my hair tightened as I continued to pleasure him.

As I moved my mouth up and down his length, I felt a sense of pride and satisfaction in knowing that I was the one bringing him this pleasure. His hands guided my movements, urging me to take him deeper and faster. Our connection grew stronger as I devoted myself to his pleasure, feeling his body tense and shudder in response to my touch.

Just as I sensed that Alex was nearing the edge, he gently pulled me away from him, a look of love and adoration in his eyes, he whispered, "I want to feel all of you," his voice thick with desire. I nodded in agreement, my heart pounding in anticipation of what was to come.

He shifted his position on the couch, sitting up straight and patting his lap, inviting me to straddle him. I moved to climb on top of him, feeling a newfound sense of confidence and desire to take control. As I positioned myself over him, I could feel the tip of his erection teasing my entrance, causing my breath to hitch in anticipation.

"Are you ready, baby?" Alex asked, his voice husky and filled with lust.

"Yes," I breathed out, my body aching for him.

I slowly lowered myself onto him, feeling his length filling me inch by inch, and we both let out deep, guttural moans of pleasure. The sensation was exquisite, and I took a moment to savor the feeling of being so intimately connected to Alex.

Our eyes locked, and I started to rock my hips slowly, feeling the delicious friction as I moved against him. Alex's hands slid up my sides and cupped my breasts, gently kneading them as his thumbs brushed over my sensitive nipples. The sensation sent shivers down my spine, and I couldn't help but let out a soft moan.

"You feel amazing, Ava," he whispered, his voice strained with desire.

Encouraged by his words, I increased the pace of my movements, grinding myself against him and eliciting more groans and moans from both of us. Our breaths grew heavier, punctuated by gasps and sighs as our bodies moved together, consumed by our passion.

As I continued to ride him, our movements becoming more urgent, I could feel the first tremors of pleasure beginning to build within me. My breath hitched, and I pressed my hands against his strong chest for support, my nails digging into his flesh as I tried to hold back my climax.

But it was no use. My body betrayed me, and I felt myself shatter around him, a wave of ecstasy washing over me, and I cried out his name, my voice raw with emotion. Alex's arms wrapped around me, holding me close as I rode out the aftershocks of my orgasm.

I rested my forehead against his, our breaths mingling as we caught our breath, but I was far from done. I locked eyes with him, a determined glint in my gaze, and I whispered, "I want more."

Alex's eyes widened in surprise, but the lustful glint in his eyes told me he was more than willing. I began to move my hips again, building up a steady rhythm as I focused on the sensations coursing through my body.

My hands roamed over his chest, tracing the contours of his muscles and the tattoos that adorned his skin, each touch sending jolts of pleasure through me. As I found the perfect angle, I felt the coil of pleasure within me begin to tighten again, and I knew I was close to another climax.

This time, however, I was determined to bring Alex with me. I leaned forward, pressing my breasts against his face, and he eagerly captured one of my nipples in his mouth, his tongue flicking and teasing it. The combination of his mouth on my breast and the feel of him inside me was almost overwhelming, and I could feel my body responding with growing intensity.

With each movement, each thrust, our passion intensified, and I could feel myself nearing the edge once more. My moans grew louder and more desperate, my body shaking with the effort of holding back my release.

"Alex, I'm so close," I gasped, my voice barely more than a whisper.

"Me too, Ava," he responded, his voice thick with arousal.

Determined to reach our peak together, I increased my pace, my body quivering with need. Alex continued to lavish attention on my breasts, alternating between them as he sucked, licked, and nibbled on my sensitive nipples.

The room was filled with the sounds of our moans, our breaths, and the wet sounds of our bodies colliding. The coil within me tightened even further, and I knew I couldn't hold back any longer.

With a final, desperate cry, I reached my climax again, my body convulsing around Alex as pleasure surged through me. The sensation pushed him over the edge as well, and he groaned my name as he released inside me, our bodies shuddering together in the throes of ecstasy.

We held onto each other tightly, our bodies slick with sweat and still trembling from the intensity of our lovemaking. As our breaths began to slow and our heartbeats returned to normal, I pressed my lips to his in a gentle, tender kiss.

We stayed like that for what felt like an eternity, wrapped in each other's arms and basking in the afterglow of our passionate encounter. It was a moment I never wanted to end, a testament to the powerful connection we shared, and a promise of the love that was growing between us.

Chapter 10

Ava

I was walking to my motorcycle after work, eager to get home and relax after a long day. It was late at night, and the Boneyard Brotherhood's clubhouse was unusually quiet, with most of the bikers having already left. As I approached my bike, I felt a prickling sensation on the back of my neck. It was as if someone was watching me, and I couldn't shake the feeling. I quickly surveyed the area, but saw no one. Chalking it up to my overactive imagination, I continued to my motorcycle.

As I reached my bike, I noticed a figure lingering nearby. My heart raced as I recognized him. It was Derek, an old boyfriend from my time in the military. He had become obsessed with me, to the point where it had become uncomfortable and dangerous. I hadn't seen him in years, but the thought of him still sent shivers down my spine.

"What are you doing here, Derek?" I asked, trying to keep my voice steady and calm.

He smirked, his dark eyes filled with an unsettling intensity. "I've been keeping an eye on you, Ava. I've missed you."

I swallowed hard, my mind racing as I tried to figure out how to handle the situation. I knew I had to remain composed, but my heart was pounding in my chest.

"Leave me alone, Derek. It's over. It's been over for years." I told him firmly, refusing to let him intimidate me.

He pushed himself off my motorcycle and stepped towards me, his face inches from mine. "You don't get to decide that," he whispered menacingly. "You belong to me, Ava. Always have, always will."

I clenched my fists, trying to control my anger and fear. "No, I don't, Derek. I never belonged to you, and I never will. What we had is in the past, and I want nothing to do with you now."

Derek laughed darkly. "You still think you have a choice, don't you? You're so naive. You think you can leave me, but you can't. You'll always be mine, and I'll do whatever it takes to make sure you understand that."

Feeling cornered and threatened, I decided to stand my ground. "You're wrong, Derek. I don't belong to anyone but myself. And if you don't leave me alone, I won't hesitate to defend myself."

His eyes narrowed, and the air around us seemed to grow colder. "Is that so?" he challenged, his voice low and dangerous.

Before I could react, he grabbed my arm, his grip like a vice. I tried to pull away, but he held me tight, causing me to cry out in pain. Refusing to be a victim, I used my free hand to strike him in the face, hoping to break free from his grasp. But Derek only tightened his grip, making me wince.

The sound of my distress echoed through the empty parking lot, drawing the attention of Alex and Cole, who had been inside the club-house.

"What's going on here?" Alex demanded, his voice cold and unyielding as he rushed towards us.

Derek's expression shifted from menacing to defensive. "This is between Ava and me. Stay out of it."

Cole scoffed, crossing his arms. "I don't think so, buddy."

I could see the tension in Alex's body as he stepped closer to Derek. "Let her go. She doesn't want anything to do with you," he warned, his tone deadly.

Derek hesitated for a moment, his eyes darting between me and the two men who had come to my rescue. Finally, he released his grip on my arm and backed away.

"I'll be watching you, Ava," Derek warned as he retreated, his eyes never leaving mine. "You can't run from me forever."

I rubbed my sore arm, trying to ignore the fear and anger that coursed through me. Alex and Cole moved to stand between Derek and me, their protective stances making it clear that they wouldn't let him hurt me.

"Get out of here," Alex ordered, his voice steely. "If I ever see you near Ava again, I won't hesitate to teach you a lesson."

Derek glared at us for a moment longer before finally turning and disappearing into the darkness. The adrenaline that had been pumping through me began to subside, leaving me feeling shaken and vulnerable.

"Are you okay, Ava?" Cole asked, his voice filled with concern as he turned to face me.

I nodded, but my voice wavered as I spoke. "Yeah, I think so. Thanks for stepping in. I don't know what he would have done if you hadn't been here."

"We've got your back, Ava," Alex assured me, his blue eyes filled with a fierce protectiveness. "No one messes with one of our own."

I smiled weakly, grateful for their support. "I appreciate it. I don't know how he found me, but I don't want him anywhere near me."

"We'll make sure he doesn't come back," Cole promised, his expression hardening. "You don't have to worry about him."

Alex placed a gentle hand on my shoulder, his touch both comforting and reassuring. "Come on, let's get you inside. You don't need to be alone right now."

I followed them back into the clubhouse, my heart still racing from the confrontation. As we entered the warm, familiar space, I realized just how much I had come to rely on the Boneyard Brotherhood. They were more than just friends—they were my family, and I knew that they would do whatever it took to keep me safe.

That night, as I lay in bed, I couldn't help but think about Derek and the danger he posed. But despite my fear, I knew that with Alex and the rest of the Boneyard Brotherhood by my side, I would never be alone in facing him.

·

Chapter 11

Alex

I couldn't help but feel uneasy as the Boneyard Brotherhood and the Night Prowlers gathered around the table, discussing the details of the heist we were planning. It wasn't like us to get involved in something so risky, but we had our reasons, and we couldn't back out now.

Ava stood beside me, her green eyes filled with concern as she listened to Ted and the Night Prowlers' leader, Razor, discussing the plan. I knew she was feeling the same misgivings I was, but we had to be strong for the sake of our friends and family.

"Alright, let's go over the plan again," Ted said, pointing at the blueprint spread out on the table. "The target is a warehouse filled with high-end electronics. We'll be hitting it during the shift change when security is at its weakest."

Razor nodded in agreement. "We've got a small window of opportunity. We need to be in and out within thirty minutes, max. Any longer and we risk getting caught."

Wilson chimed in, "We'll need to split into teams. One team handles the entrance and security, while the other team takes care of the actual heist."

Sid suggested, "Cole can lead the security team. He has the experience and know-how to keep things under control."

Razor looked over at Ava and me. "You two are our best bet for the inside job. Alex, your special forces training will come in handy, and Ava, your combat skills are invaluable. You up for this?"

I glanced at Ava, and she gave me a slight nod. "We're in," I confirmed, my voice steady despite the knot of anxiety forming in my stomach.

Ted continued, "We'll need a few more people on the inside to help load the merchandise onto the trucks. Chase and Tara, you're in."

Chase nodded, his face set in a determined expression. "We won't let you down."

Maddie, who had been listening intently, raised her hand. "What about me? I can help with the getaway vehicles."

Ted smiled approvingly. "Good idea, Maddie. You and Van Cleef will handle that."

Razor took a deep breath before laying out the final details. "Once we have everything loaded, we'll rendezvous at the designated spot, and from there, we'll take the merchandise. It's important that we stick to the plan and keep our communication lines open."

As we continued discussing the details and ironing out the plan, I couldn't help but steal glances at Ava. She was so strong and brave, and I couldn't help but admire her resilience. But I also knew that she was worried about what we were getting ourselves into.

After the meeting wrapped up, Ava and I found ourselves alone in a quiet corner of the clubhouse. The tension between us had been building over the past few days, and as we stood there, inches apart, I could feel it reaching a breaking point. I couldn't help but reach out and gently tuck a stray lock of her dark hair behind her ear. Our eyes locked, and for a moment, the world around us seemed to fade away.

Ava's breath hitched, and she closed the distance between us, pressing her soft lips against mine. The kiss was tender and filled with unspoken emotion. I wrapped my arms around her, pulling her closer to me, reveling in the warmth and comfort that she brought me in such uncertain times.

We reluctantly broke apart, our foreheads resting against each other as we caught our breath. I could see the concern in her eyes, and I knew we needed to address the issue that had been haunting us both.

"Ava," I said softly, "I know we both have our misgivings about this heist, but I need to know that you'll be with me, no matter what happens."

She nodded, determination shining in her eyes. "Of course, Alex. We'll stick together. As always, I'll watch your back, and you watch mine."

I couldn't help but smile, grateful for her unwavering support. "Alright, then. Let's make sure we understand our roles in this heist. I'll be keeping an eye on the Night Prowlers while you handle the security system."

She nodded again, her expression serious. "I've got it. And once we're in, we'll stay in contact, so we know what's happening at all times."

Our conversation about the heist naturally led to the issue that had been haunting us both. "Ava, about Derek..." I began hesitantly, not sure how to put my thoughts into words.

She nodded, her eyes filled with a mix of fear and determination. "I know, Alex. I can't stop thinking about him either. The fact that he's stalking me now... it's terrifying. But we can't let him control our lives. We'll deal with him, together."

I tightened my embrace, grateful for her support and strength. "You're right. I just can't shake this feeling that he's not done with us yet. We need to stay vigilant, protect each other."

Ava smiled softly, her green eyes filled with love and loyalty. "We always have each other's backs, Alex. That's what makes us strong. We'll face whatever comes our way, together."

Chapter 12

Ava

The night of the heist was upon us, and the tension in the air was palpable. The Boneyard Brotherhood and the Night Prowlers were dressed in black, their faces covered by masks to protect their identities. The warehouse we were targeting loomed in the distance, a beacon of temptation and danger.

As we gathered around the trucks, I couldn't help but steal a glance at Alex. He looked every bit the fearless leader, his broad shoulders set with determination. Our eyes met for a moment, and he gave me a reassuring nod, his blue eyes filled with a silent promise to keep me safe.

The heist began as planned, with Cole's team expertly disabling the security cameras and creating a safe entrance for us. Alex and I, along with Chase and Tara, stealthily made our way into the warehouse, our hearts pounding with anticipation.

As we approached the rows of high-end electronics, Alex leaned in close to me, his voice barely above a whisper. "Remember, Ava, we need to work fast. Keep an eye on your surroundings, and let me know if anything seems off."

I nodded, my mind racing with both excitement and fear. "Got it. You watch my back, and I'll watch yours."

We split up, each of us quickly filling our bags with the valuable merchandise. The silence in the warehouse was deafening, the only sounds being the quiet rustling of our movements and the distant hum of the machinery.

Suddenly, I heard a commotion from the direction of the entrance. It sounded like shouting and the unmistakable crack of gunfire. Panic rose in my chest as I realized that something had gone terribly wrong.

I reached for my walkie-talkie, my voice trembling. "Alex, we've got trouble. It sounds like the security team is under attack."

His voice came through the speaker, filled with urgency. "Ava, meet me at our rendezvous point. We need to get out of here now."

I hurried through the maze of electronics, my heart pounding in my ears. As I turned the corner, I saw Alex waiting for me, his eyes filled with concern. "Are you okay?" he asked, his voice barely audible over the sounds of chaos outside.

I nodded, my grip tightening on my bag of stolen goods. "I'm fine, but we need to get out of here before we're caught in the crossfire."

We moved quickly through the warehouse, our eyes scanning the area for any sign of danger. The sound of the gunfire was getting closer, and I could feel the adrenaline surging through me, urging me to run faster.

As we reached the exit, we were met with a horrifying sight. Cole's team had been ambushed, and they were locked in a fierce firefight with an unknown group of attackers.

Without hesitation, Alex grabbed my arm, pulling me behind a nearby stack of crates for cover. "We need to find another way out," he whispered, his eyes darting around the chaotic scene.

I nodded, my mind racing as I tried to think of an escape route. "There's a back exit on the other side of the warehouse. If we can make it there, we might be able to slip out unnoticed."

With our plan in place, we made a mad dash for the other side of the warehouse, avoiding the firefight as best as we could. Just as we reached the back exit, a stray bullet whizzed through the air, hitting Alex in the shoulder.

I gasped in horror as he stumbled, his face contorted in pain. "Alex!" I cried, my heart seizing in fear for his life.

He gritted his teeth, trying to hide his agony. "I'm okay, Ava. It's just a flesh wound. We need to keep moving."

Despite the pain, Alex pushed himself to keep going, and I couldn't help but admire his strength and determination. We slipped out of the back exit and into the darkness, our breaths coming in ragged gasps as we put as much distance between us and the warehouse as possible.

As we reached the safety of a nearby alley, I finally allowed myself to fully assess Alex's injury. The blood was seeping through his shirt, and I knew we needed to act quickly to stop the bleeding.

"Let me take a look at it," I said softly, my voice filled with concern.

Alex nodded, his face pale as he leaned against the cold brick wall. I carefully removed his jacket and cut away his shirt, exposing the wound. It was a clean shot, and I knew that he was lucky it hadn't hit anything vital.

"Okay, this is going to hurt, but we need to clean the wound and stop the bleeding," I warned him, my hands shaking slightly as I reached for my first aid kit.

I cleaned the wound as gently as I could, wincing in sympathy as Alex hissed in pain. Once it was clean, I applied pressure to stop the bleeding and wrapped a bandage tightly around his shoulder.

"Thank you," he murmured, his voice weak but filled with gratitude. "I owe you one, Ava."

I shook my head, the weight of the night's events heavy on my shoulders. "No, we're in this together, remember? Now let's get out of here and regroup with the others."

We made our way back to the clubhouse, our minds reeling from the night's events. We didn't know who had attacked us or why, but one thing was certain: our lives had just gotten a whole lot more dangerous.

As we gathered with the rest of our team, nursing our wounds and trying to make sense of the chaos, I couldn't help but feel a renewed sense of camaraderie. We had faced the worst together and survived. And now, more than ever, we needed to stick together if we were going to uncover the truth behind the attack and protect ourselves from further harm.

Chapter 13

Ava

The air was thick with tension as the Boneyard Brotherhood gathered around the table, trying to make sense of the disastrous heist and the Night Prowlers' betrayal. After everything we had gone through to broker peace between our clubs, it felt like a slap in the face. We had been played, and now we needed to figure out our next move.

Ted slammed his fist on the table, his face a mixture of anger and frustration. "Damn it! We put our necks on the line for those bastards, and this is how they repay us?"

Wilson chimed in, his voice filled with bitterness. "They used us from the start. We never should have trusted them."

Van Cleef shook his head, his face grim. "It's hard to believe that Razor and his crew were playing us all along. We need to find out their true intentions and why they set us up."

Sid leaned back in his chair, his eyes clouded with worry. "Not to mention the group that ambushed us during the heist. Who the hell were they?"

Chase spoke up, his voice steady and determined. "We need to gather as much information as we can. Find out who those attackers were, and what the Night Prowlers' real endgame is."

Tara nodded in agreement, her expression serious. "And we need to be careful. They'll be expecting us to retaliate, so we need to stay one step ahead."

Dylan, who had been listening intently, added, "We also need to make sure everyone is safe. We don't know how far the Night Prowlers will go to keep their secrets."

Cole's deep voice cut through the discussion. "We can't let them get away with this. We need to come up with a plan and hit them back, hard."

Ted looked around the room, his eyes meeting each of ours in turn. "We're all in agreement, then. We're going to find out the truth behind the Night Prowlers' betrayal, and we're going to make sure they pay for what they've done."

There was a murmur of assent around the table, and I couldn't help but glance at Alex. His jaw was set, his blue eyes hard with resolve. I knew he was as determined as the rest of us to get to the bottom of this and protect the Boneyard Brotherhood at all costs.

Ted cleared his throat before addressing us. "Alright, let's break down our plan of action. We need to gather intel, prepare for possible retaliation, and ensure everyone's safety."

Wilson raised his hand. "First off, we need to infiltrate the Night Prowlers' ranks. We need someone on the inside who can feed us information about their plans and any potential weaknesses."

Van Cleef nodded. "Agreed. But who do we send? It needs to be someone who can blend in and avoid suspicion."

Before anyone else could make a suggestion, I spoke up, surprising Alex. "I'll do it. I'll find a way to get close to them and relay any intel back to the club."

Ted considered my offer for a moment, and then nodded. "Ava, I trust your judgment. If you believe you can handle this, I support your decision."

Cole interjected with concern, "I don't like the idea of Ava going in alone. The Night Prowlers are dangerous. Maybe we should consider teaming up with another biker club to take them on. They must have other enemies."

Ted stroked his beard thoughtfully. "It's worth exploring, but we need to be cautious about who we trust. For now, let's proceed with Ava's infiltration. We'll also look into potential alliances."

Sid chimed in, "While Ava is gathering information, we should also work on strengthening our own defenses. We don't know when or how the Night Prowlers might strike, so we need to be prepared."

Chase added, "That means fortifying the clubhouse, setting up surveillance, and being prepared for anything they might throw at us."

Ted nodded, pleased with the suggestions. "Alright, that's a solid plan. Cole, you and Dylan will be in charge of the fortifications. I want this place to be a fortress."

Cole and Dylan exchanged a determined look and nodded, ready to take on the responsibility. "You got it, Ted. We won't let you down."

The discussion continued to flow, with each member contributing ideas and taking on responsibilities. Wilson and Sid volunteered to reach out to other biker clubs, searching for potential allies to help us fight against the Night Prowlers.

Cole, growing increasingly agitated, slammed his fist on the table. "We can't just sit back and wait for Ava to infiltrate the Night Prowlers. We need to hit them hard, and we need to do it soon!"

Ted looked at Cole, understanding his anger but maintaining a level-headed approach. "I understand your frustration, Cole, but we need to be strategic. We'll be ready to strike when the time is right, and with Ava on the inside, we'll have the upper hand."

As the meeting progressed, the air of determination grew stronger. Despite the betrayal and uncertainty, the Boneyard Brotherhood stood united, ready to face whatever challenges lay ahead.

"I know things seem grim right now," Ted said, looking around the table at the faces of our club members, "but I have faith in each and every one of you. We've faced tough times before, and we've always come out stronger. Let's show the Night Prowlers and anyone else who threatens us that they picked the wrong club to mess with."

A resounding chorus of agreement echoed through the room, and the members dispersed to begin their assigned tasks. Though the road ahead was uncertain, one thing was clear: the Boneyard Brotherhood wouldn't go down without a fight.

Later, after the meeting had adjourned, Alex and I found ourselves sitting together outside the clubhouse, the cool night air enveloping us. We both needed a moment away from the charged atmosphere inside.

"So," Alex began hesitantly, his voice barely above a whisper, "how are you really feeling about all of this? The betrayal, my injury, and your decision to infiltrate the Night Prowlers?"

I sighed, rubbing my temples. "Honestly, Alex, I'm scared. But I'm also angry. The Night Prowlers crossed a line, and we need to do whatever it takes to make sure they don't get away with it."

Alex's face hardened. "Ava, I understand wanting to hit them back, but you volunteering to go undercover with them? It's too dangerous. There must be another way."

I looked him in the eyes, my own determination shining through. "Alex, I can't stand by and do nothing while the people I care about, like you, get hurt. I need to do this, not just for the club, but for us."

His jaw clenched, and I could see the frustration and fear in his eyes. "You saw what happened to me. I was lucky it wasn't worse. I can't bear the thought of something happening to you, Ava."

Our voices had risen, and the strain of the situation was beginning to show on our faces. We argued back and forth, the tension between us growing.

"I know it's risky, but I believe I can do this. I'm strong, Alex. I'm not going to let them break me."

He shook his head, clearly not convinced. "You're strong, Ava, but even the strongest people can be broken by circumstances like these. What if they suspect you? What if they find out you're working against them? I don't think I could handle losing you."

I slammed my fist on the table, my frustration spilling over. "And what if we don't do anything and more people get hurt? What if they go after someone else we love? What if they come for you again, Alex? I can't stand the thought of that either!"

Alex rubbed his face with his hands, trying to find the right words. "I get it, Ava, I do. But I can't help but feel like there's got to be another way, one that doesn't put you in so much danger."

"Maybe there is, but we can't afford to wait around and hope for the best. We need to act, and I'm willing to take this risk for the club, and for you."

Our argument continued, neither of us willing to back down. The betrayal, Alex's injury, and my decision were all putting a strain on our relationship.

Finally, Alex sighed, defeated. "Promise me you'll be careful, Ava. Promise me you'll come back to me."

"I promise," I whispered, tears streaming down my face. "I'll do everything in my power to keep myself safe while getting the intel we need."

As the night wore on, we returned to the clubhouse, preparing ourselves for the challenges that lay ahead. Our lives had changed in the blink of an eye, but we were determined to persevere.

Chapter 14

Alex

The meeting room was buzzing with tension, thick and palpable. We, the Boneyard Brotherhood, were seated together, our faces etched with grim determination. My injured shoulder ached, a stinging reminder of the recent betrayal. My gaze wandered to Ava, her bravery radiating from her as she silently mulled over the implications of her proposed undercover mission to infiltrate the Night Prowlers.

Sid, our resident mechanic and a reliable ally, had been fostering an alliance with another biker club, one which had their own bone to pick with the Night Prowlers. He had word from them, a proposal that had the potential to change the direction of our campaign.

Ted, our revered leader, broke the silence, his voice firm. "Alright, Sid, out with it. What's their proposal?"

Sid cleared his throat, his voice steady as he relayed the message. "They propose a sneak attack. Quick, direct, and brutal. They're gathering intel on the Prowlers' base locations and their weak spots."

Van Cleef, the club's charmer, contemplated aloud, his voice echoing around the room. "It's an interesting plan, but I think we shouldn't discard the thought of a covert operation. If we can infiltrate them, understand their operations, it might give us a significant advantage."

The room fell silent as everyone absorbed Van Cleef's words. Ava, the center of the undercover plan, was quiet, her eyes reflecting her inner turmoil. I couldn't help but worry for her safety, her courage notwith-standing.

Ted looked around the room, his gaze piercing each of us as he weighed our opinions. "What do you guys think? Should we opt for the surprise attack or stick with the original plan of infiltration?"

Wilson, Ted's right-hand man, was quick to respond. "Infiltration is my choice. It might be a slow process, but the insights we get could tip the scales in our favor."

Cole, our enforcer, and a man of action, had a different viewpoint. "I think the sneak attack is our best bet. We know how ruthless the Night Prowlers are, a swift, unexpected hit could be just the thing to knock them off balance."

The room erupted into a heated debate, each one voicing their thoughts and concerns. Amidst the noise, my eyes kept straying to Ava, the thought of her risking her life in enemy territory gnawing at me. I saw her eyes flicker towards me, her silent nod of understanding serving as reassurance.

Feeling a sudden surge of resolve, I decided to speak up. "I agree with Cole," I started, my voice firm. "A sneak attack has its advantages. Ava, you're brave, and I have no doubt you'd excel at undercover work. But the risks... I don't want you in the line of fire."

Ava turned to me, her eyes full of understanding. "I get it, Alex. But remember, I signed up for this."

Before I could respond, Ted's authoritative voice cut through the tension. "Enough! We'll go with the sneak attack. We need to end this. If that fails, we'll move to the infiltration plan. Sid, keep the other club informed. "

The room emptied out slowly, members of the Boneyard Brother-hood filing out one by one, their faces etched with the grim promise of the upcoming conflict. Ava, however, stood rooted to the spot, her usual spark dimmed, her face a mask of contemplation and unease.

"Ava," I ventured, sidling up to her, my heart heavy with concern. "You're a million miles away. It's the alliance, isn't it?"

She pivoted to face me, the worry in her emerald eyes more profound than I had anticipated. "It's more than just that, Alex. It feels like... like you've stopped believing in me."

Confusion coursed through me, followed by a surge of indignation. "That's preposterous, Ava. I—"

"You championed the sneak attack instead of my plan for infiltration," she interrupted, her tone laced with a bitterness that stung. "There was no deliberation, no consultation. You just decided."

Frustration welled up inside me. "I was only trying to keep you safe, Ava!" I argued, my temper flaring. "When I saw an opportunity to keep you out of the line of fire, I took it."

Her stare was icy, her anger palpable. "By declaring war? Do you understand the implications, Alex? This strategy could jeopardize us all! We're essentially marching blindfolded into the lion's den!"

I swallowed hard, her words cutting deep. But my resolve remained. "Ava, I would rather confront danger head-on than let you walk into a trap on some stealth mission."

Her expression softened minutely, but there was an unyielding resolve in her gaze. "Alex, I can look after myself. I've proven that repeatedly. I don't need a knight in shining armor."

My heart pounded in my chest as I met her gaze. "I know, Ava," I conceded, my voice barely a whisper. "But knowing doesn't ease my worry. It doesn't change the fact that I care about you—deeply. And the mere thought of you in danger..."

A tense silence fell between us, her gaze never leaving mine. Then, with a sigh, she said, "I care about you too, Alex. But we can't let our personal feelings cloud our judgment. We need to trust each other. We're in this together."

I nodded, guilt and regret washing over me. "I should've consulted you. I apologize, Ava. Truly."

She offered a small nod in return, an acknowledgment of my apology. "We'll overcome this, Alex. Together."

With a sudden move, Ava stepped closer, her eyes burning into mine. Her breath hitched, a barely audible gasp that nevertheless sent a shiver coursing through me. In response, I gently pulled her towards me, our bodies aligning in a familiar dance of intimacy. Her eyes fluttered closed as our lips met, the kiss a salve to the heated words that had passed between us.

This wasn't a kiss of appeasement, but one of raw emotion—fear, longing, desire—all intermingling in a feverish dance. I cradled her face in my hands, my thumbs tracing the curve of her cheeks, the heat of her skin searing into my fingertips. Ava's hands traveled up to my shoulders, her fingers grazing over my injured shoulder, a gentle touch that soothed the pain.

As the kiss deepened, I moved my hands down to her waist, pulling her closer until there was no space left between us. She responded in kind, her fingers tangling in my hair, tugging gently in a move that elicited a low growl from me. The world outside the room ceased to exist; all that mattered was Ava and the fire that ignited between us.

Ava broke the kiss first, her chest heaving as she tried to catch her breath. But instead of pulling away, she leaned her forehead against mine, her breath fanning over my face. Her hands were still in my hair, her body pressed against mine. There was a moment of silence before she spoke. "Alex," she murmured, her voice barely audible.

"Yes, Ava?" I responded, my voice equally low.

"We can't let this fight tear us apart. We need to stick together."

I nodded, brushing my thumb against her lower lip. "I know, Ava. I'm sorry. I should have trusted you."

She looked at me then, her eyes softening. "And I should have understood your concerns. Just promise to communicate better, Alex. For us."

I nodded, pressing a soft kiss to her forehead. "For us," I echoed.

A quiet nod was her response, her consent given as she pulled me closer, her hands moving from my hair to grip the fabric of my shirt. I reciprocated, my hands tracing the curve of her waist, feeling the warmth of her skin through her clothes. There was a subtle shift, a silent understanding that passed between us as we teetered on the precipice of something more.

The room around us seemed to fade, the weight of the upcoming battle momentarily forgotten as our world narrowed down to just the two of us. The distance between our bodies disappeared as I pulled her closer, my hands splaying across the small of her back, pulling her flush against me.

"Alex," she whispered, her voice barely audible as she tilted her head back, offering me better access to the delicate line of her throat. The sight of her vulnerability and trust stirred something deep within me, making my heart pound with a fierce, possessive desire.

I dipped my head, pressing soft kisses along her throat, eliciting a soft sigh from her. The sound sent a thrill of satisfaction through me, encouraging me to explore further. My hands moved from her back to her sides, tracing the curve of her body over her clothes before making their way to the hem of her shirt.

Our lips met again in a searing kiss, slower this time, but no less passionate. My fingers slipped under her shirt, grazing the warm, soft skin of her lower back, tracing a path upwards. She gasped against my lips, a soft sound that was swallowed by our kiss, her fingers digging into my shoulders.

Pulling away from the kiss, I met her eyes, silently asking for her permission to continue. She nodded, her eyes heavy with desire and trust. A smile tugged at the corners of her mouth, a silent encouragement that made my heart pound louder in my chest. I took a moment to appreciate her, the way her chest heaved, the flush that spread across her cheeks, the desire that clouded her eyes.

Slowly, with her assistance, I lifted her shirt over her head, revealing the beauty that lay beneath. Her skin glowed in the dim light of the room, a sight that took my breath away. My hands moved to cup her face, my thumbs tracing her cheekbones as I looked into her eyes. "You're beautiful, Ava," I murmured, my voice husky with emotion.

A blush spread across her cheeks, but she didn't look away. "So are you, Alex," she said, her voice barely above a whisper.

I leaned in and placed a soft kiss on her collarbone, my hands trailing down to the button of her jeans. She watched me, her breath hitching as I slowly unbuttoned and unzipped her pants. A soft gasp escaped her lips as I slid them down her legs, taking her underwear with them. She stood before me, completely exposed, and I was momentarily awestruck by her beauty.

My gaze roamed over her body, drinking in every detail. Her chest rose and fell with each shallow breath she took, her skin glistening with a thin sheen of sweat. She looked at me with an expression of pure trust, her hands reaching out to grip my shoulders.

As I sank to my knees, my hands on her hips for support, I allowed my gaze to travel up her body, from her bare feet, over her long, slender legs, to the point where they met. She was already flushed, her eyes a darker green now, her chest rising and falling with each quick breath she took. A sense of awe washed over me. I was about to worship her, to show her the depth of my emotions that words could not express.

Drawing in a calming breath, I leaned in, my lips brushing the soft skin of her inner thigh. She shivered, her fingers tangling in my hair as I pressed a trail of soft kisses higher. I listened to her breathing, feeling it hitch when I moved closer to her center. It was a dance of anticipation and desire, a dance only she and I were privy to.

Pausing, I looked up at her. Ava's gaze met mine, her eyes pleading and full of trust. It was the silent affirmation I needed. I returned my attention to the task at hand, my breath ghosting over her most intimate area.

She gasped softly, her grip on my hair tightening as I pressed the first tender kiss to her. I took my time, each brush of my lips against her designed to elicit a response. The taste of her on my tongue was intoxicating, the soft whimpers escaping her lips spurring me on.

Ava's body writhed under my touch, her legs trembling as I explored her with my tongue. I traced every fold, every hidden secret, my every move slow and deliberate. I was not rushing this; I wanted her to feel every sensation, every wave of pleasure.

Her soft cries grew louder, her body arching into me as I quickened my pace. I could feel her nearing the edge, her hands gripping my hair tighter, her breath coming in sharp gasps. I persisted, determined to bring her over the edge. I looked up, watching her face contort in pleasure, her eyes shut tight, her lips parted. It was the most beautiful sight I'd ever seen.

The moment she crested, her body tensing before going slack, her quiet cry echoing in the room, was one of the most profound moments of my life. I stayed where I was, allowing her to ride out the waves of pleasure, my hands soothing over her hips and thighs.

Only when her breathing started to even out, did I rise to my feet, pressing a soft kiss to her belly before capturing her lips in a slow, heated kiss. The taste of her on my lips sent a jolt of desire through me, reigniting the flame that had been momentarily quelled.

Ava's heated skin against mine felt electric, the spark between us reignited with a vengeance. My hands roamed her body, memorizing every curve, every dip, even as her fingers busied themselves with the fastening of my jeans.

Once rid of the last piece of fabric separating us, I lifted her with ease, her legs instinctively wrapping around my waist. Her back pressed against the cool wall of the room, a stark contrast to the heat radiating off us. Her arms linked around my neck, pulling me in closer, and her breath hitched when I pressed into her.

"Alex..." she moaned, her fingers grazing over the nape of my neck, sending shivers down my spine.

"Are you okay?" I asked, my voice strained with desire, yet laced with concern.

Her eyes met mine, blazing with the same intense passion I felt coursing through my veins. "Never been better," she replied, her voice a sultry whisper that pushed me beyond any restraint I had left.

With her approval, I began to move, establishing a slow, deliberate rhythm that had her back arching against the cold wall. Each thrust drew a soft whimper from her, the sweetest melody to my ears. "Alex...," she moaned again, the sound of my name on her lips fuelling my desire.

"You're so stunning, Ava," I breathed, my voice rough with passion. "I love seeing you like this. Just for me."

Her fingers dug into my shoulders, a silent plea for more. I gladly obliged, picking up the pace, losing myself in her. Her moans echoed through the room, each one a testament to the connection we shared.

My name slipped from her lips like a prayer, her body arching against mine as she succumbed to the overwhelming pleasure. "Oh, Alex... I...," she gasped, her words dissolving into incoherent moans.

Her pleasure tipped me over the edge, our bodies shuddering in unison as we climaxed together. "Ava..." I groaned, my voice a low growl filled with raw emotion.

As our breaths slowed, Ava's eyes fluttered open, meeting mine. Her gaze was soft, full of love, and in that moment, I knew we were stronger together. As I gently lowered her back onto her feet, I pressed my forehead against hers.

Our bodies were tangled together, a beautiful mess of shared heat and affection. Our argument seemed a world away, our connection stronger than ever. In the aftermath of our shared intimacy, we found our strength – a strength that would carry us into the impending battle and beyond. Together.

Chapter 15

Ava

The sun was beginning to set as I watched the Boneyard Brother-hood prepare for battle. The clubhouse was alive with the electric energy of anticipation, a stark contrast to the serene twilight painting the sky. But beneath the surface, a deep undercurrent of tension was palpable, the danger we were about to face casting a heavy shadow over us all.

The alliance was formed, an uneasy union of clubs bound by the common enemy - the Night Prowlers. The image of their smug leader, his eyes gleaming with deceptive camaraderie, still haunted me. I knew what was at stake; we all did. The threat was real, and it was coming for us.

"Hey, Ava." Alex's voice cut through my thoughts, grounding me back to the moment. His blue eyes were intent, mirroring the same concern I felt. "You ready for this?"

I took a deep breath, my eyes searching his for reassurance. There was a silent understanding between us, a shared resolve forged through trials and tribulations, and it steadied me. "As ready as I'll ever be."

His gaze softened, a warm hand reaching out to gently squeeze mine. "We're in this together, Ava. We always have been."

The determination in his voice was enough to ignite the spark of courage within me. Nodding, I reciprocated his squeeze. "Together," I echoed.

In the following days, our training became more intense, every member of the alliance pushing their limits. Alex and I trained together, our physical strengths complementing each other, our shared past in the military serving as an unspoken bond. The time we spent together only brought us closer, the lingering tension between us gradually giving way to a deepening connection.

One evening, after a particularly grueling session, Alex pulled me aside. His gaze was intense, his voice uncharacteristically soft. "Ava," he said, his hand brushing against my sweaty hair, "I want you to know that no matter what happens, I'm here for you."

His words struck a chord deep within me. I knew he meant it, and I also knew that the sentiment was mutual. "And I'm here for you, Alex," I replied, my voice barely above a whisper.

His lips curled into a small, weary smile, his blue eyes glinting with a mixture of relief and affection. And in that moment, I felt a surge of emotion that was too powerful to be denied. We were in this together, bound by a force far stronger than any adversary we might face.

Despite the impending danger, the Boneyard Brotherhood was resolute. We were a family, united by more than just our love for riding. The threat against our club was a threat against each and every one of us, and we were determined to protect our own.

Van Cleef's jokes lightened the mood during our intense training sessions, his infectious laughter echoing through the clubhouse. Ted and Wilson strategized, their experienced minds working together to ensure our victory. Sid, despite his back pain, worked tirelessly on our bikes, ensuring they were in top shape for the upcoming battle. Maddie and Cindy supplied us with nourishing meals, their constant presence a comforting reminder of what we were fighting for.

In the midst of this, my bond with Alex only strengthened. Our shared moments, whether they were heated sparring sessions or quiet conversations under the stars, became a sanctuary from the chaos around us. His touch, his voice, his presence... they became my calm in the storm, a safe haven in a world teetering on the precipice of uncertainty.

The night before the fight, Alex and I found ourselves alone in the now familiar setting of our shared quarters. The air between us was thick with unspoken words, the weight of the impending battle hanging heavy in the room. His gaze met mine, a silent conversation passing between us.

"Ava," he began, his voice steady despite the tumult of emotions reflected in his eyes. "I need you to promise me something."

His serious tone made my heart skip a beat. "What is it, Alex?"

He took a step closer, his hand reaching out to gently cup my cheek. His thumb traced the curve of my jaw, his touch soothing and familiar. "Promise me you'll stay safe tomorrow."

A soft laugh escaped my lips, the irony of his request not lost on me. "I could say the same to you, Alex."

His hand tightened slightly around my cheek, his blue eyes darkening. "I'm serious, Ava. I can't... I won't lose you."

The intensity of his words left me breathless. The fear in his voice was a testament to the depth of his feelings for me, a silent confession of love that he had yet to put into words. "And I won't lose you, Alex," I murmured, my hand coming up to cover his. "We'll get through this. Together."

The tension seemed to ease out of him at my words, his hand dropping from my face to wrap around my waist, pulling me closer. "Together," he echoed, his voice barely a whisper.

As our lips met, everything else faded into the background. The impending battle, the uncertainty of the future, the fear of loss... all of it disappeared. All that mattered was the man holding me, his touch grounding me, his warmth enveloping me.

Our kiss deepened, a perfect blend of passion and desperation, of love and fear. His hands roamed over my body, each touch sending sparks of desire coursing through my veins. The world outside ceased to exist; it was just Alex and me, lost in each other.

Alex's lips trailed down my neck, sending shivers down my spine. His hands expertly untangled the knot of my training tank top, his touch leaving a blazing trail on my skin. His mouth found the sensitive spot just below my ear, his teeth grazing the skin, causing me to gasp.

He pulled back, his eyes meeting mine. There was a question in his gaze, a silent request for permission. And with a nod, I gave it to him.

That night, we found solace in each other's arms, our bodies intertwining in a dance as old as time. Our shared intimacy served as a balm for the fear and uncertainty that lingered in our hearts. Our whispered promises echoed in the room, a testament to the strength of our bond.

As I fell asleep in his arms, his steady heartbeat a soothing lullaby, I knew that no matter what the future held, we would face it together. The Boneyard Brotherhood was not just a club; it was a family. And we would fight to protect it, come hell or high water.

Chapter 16

Alex

The early morning air was cool and crisp, its freshness a stark contrast to the tension that had been building up in the Boneyard Brotherhood's clubhouse. The usually laid-back and jovial atmosphere was replaced by an undercurrent of anticipation, a shared understanding that today was the day we'd confront the Night Prowlers.

Ava walked out of the clubhouse, her wavy dark hair slicked back into a combat-ready bun. The morning sunlight highlighted the contours of her athletic, curvaceous form as she moved with purpose, her military-grade armor glinting against the light. Her vibrant green eyes were focused, a clear testament to her determination. The sight of her, fierce and battle-ready, was both awe-inspiring and gut-wrenching.

A part of me was comforted by her presence. She was strong, resilient, a warrior through and through. Yet, the thought of her in harm's way stirred a protective instinct within me that was hard to suppress. It was a conflict of emotions, a tug-of-war between my confidence in her abilities and my instinct to keep her safe.

"Alex," Van Cleef called out, his voice pulling me out of my thoughts. The usual playfulness was absent from his tone, replaced by a solemnity that matched the gravity of the situation. "We're about ready to move out."

"Give me a moment," I replied, my gaze never leaving Ava.

She was at my side now, her hand lightly resting on my arm. "You okay?" she asked, the concern in her voice almost palpable.

"Yeah," I said, giving her a small, reassuring smile. "Just... a lot on my mind."

Her eyes softened, understanding flooding her features. "We'll get through this, Alex," she said, her grip on my arm tightening. "Together."

"Together," I echoed, the word resonating within me, amplifying my resolve. I pulled her close, hugging her tightly. I took a moment to breathe her in, the scent of her acting like a soothing balm to the storm of emotions within me.

The chorus of revving engines brought me back to reality. The time had come. I gave Ava one last lingering look before climbing onto my motorcycle. Her hand found mine, her grip strong and reassuring.

The ride to Night Prowlers' territory was a blur, my mind occupied by thoughts of Ava, the impending battle, and the uncertainty that lay beyond. The clubhouse of the Night Prowlers loomed ahead, a stark reminder of the confrontation that awaited us. I glanced at Ava one more time, her face a mask of steely determination.

The attack happened swiftly, a storm unleashed upon the unsuspecting Night Prowlers. Ava and I fought shoulder to shoulder, our actions perfectly in sync as if choreographed. It was a dance of sorts, a deadly ballet where every move mattered.

In the heat of battle, I couldn't help but marvel at Ava. Her every move was a testament to her training, her resilience. She was a whirlwind of power and grace, a force of nature in her own right. Her presence was a beacon in the chaos, a guiding light that kept me grounded.

Amidst the mayhem, our eyes locked. There was a spark, a connection that transcended the battle around us. Guided by an impulse, I reached out to her, my hand gently caressing her face. Her eyes closed briefly, leaning into my touch.

In the cacophony of the battle, I found myself whispering, "I love you, Ava."

Her eyes flicked open, surprise etching her features. The battle raged on around us, but for a moment, it was just us, lost in our own world amidst the chaos.

"What did you say?" she asked, her voice barely audible above the noise.

"I said, I love you," I repeated, looking into her eyes.

Ava stared at me, the surprise in her eyes melting into something softer, something vulnerable. "Alex," she began, her voice choked with emotion.

But before she could respond, a shout rang out, pulling us back to the grim reality. We had no time for heartfelt confessions. There was a battle to be won.

With a last look at Ava, I charged back into the fray. My heart pounded in my chest, not from the adrenaline of the fight, but from the words I had just spoken. I had confessed my love for Ava amidst a battlefield, not knowing if we would live to see another day.

The battle raged on, a blur of violence and noise. But through it all, Ava was a constant presence by my side. We fought back to back, our movements synchronized as if we were one. Every time I struck down an enemy, I could feel her fighting with me, her presence as real as the battle cries around us.

Finally, after what felt like an eternity, the Night Prowlers began to retreat. We had managed to hold them off, for now. I found Ava amidst the chaos, her eyes meeting mine. We were both battered and bruised, but we were alive. We had survived.

As the dust settled, I walked over to Ava. Her eyes were wide, her breathing heavy. She looked at me, her gaze searching mine.

"Alex," she said, her voice barely a whisper. "You... you meant it? What you said during the fight?"

I reached out, tucking a loose strand of hair behind her ear. "Every word, Ava," I said, looking into her eyes. "I love you."

Ava looked at me, her eyes filling with tears. And then, she was in my arms, her body shaking as she sobbed. I held her, my heart aching for her. We had survived the battle, but the war was far from over. But as long as we were together, I knew we could face anything.

With the smell of smoke and gunpowder still thick in the air, I held Ava close, our hearts beating in sync amidst the chaos. The world around us may have been in shambles, but in that moment, holding Ava in my arms, I felt a sense of peace. Because despite the chaos, despite the danger we were in, one thing was clear to me.

I loved Ava, and I would do anything to protect her. And as I held her in my arms, I made a silent vow to myself. No matter what happened, no matter how dangerous things got, I would keep Ava safe. Because she was more than just my fellow warrior, more than a fellow member of the Boneyard Brotherhood.

She was the woman I loved. And I would go through hell and back for her.

Chapter 17

Alex

The early morning air was cool and crisp, its freshness a stark contrast to the tension that had been building up in the Boneyard Brotherhood's clubhouse. The usually laid-back and jovial atmosphere was replaced by an undercurrent of anticipation, a shared understanding that today was the day we'd confront the Night Prowlers.

Ava walked out of the clubhouse, her wavy dark hair slicked back into a combat-ready bun. The morning sunlight highlighted the contours of her athletic, curvaceous form as she moved with purpose, her military-grade armor glinting against the light. Her vibrant green eyes were focused, a clear testament to her determination. The sight of her, fierce and battle-ready, was both awe-inspiring and gut-wrenching.

A part of me was comforted by her presence. She was strong, resilient, a warrior through and through. Yet, the thought of her in harm's way stirred a protective instinct within me that was hard to suppress. It was a conflict of emotions, a tug-of-war between my confidence in her abilities and my instinct to keep her safe.

"Alex," Van Cleef called out, his voice pulling me out of my thoughts. The usual playfulness was absent from his tone, replaced by a solemnity that matched the gravity of the situation. "We're about ready to move out."

"Give me a moment," I replied, my gaze never leaving Ava.

She was at my side now, her hand lightly resting on my arm. "You okay?" she asked, the concern in her voice almost palpable.

"Yeah," I said, giving her a small, reassuring smile.

Her eyes softened, understanding flooding her features. "We'll get through this, Alex," she said, her grip on my arm tightening. "Together."

"Together," I echoed, the word resonating within me, amplifying my resolve. I pulled her close, hugging her tightly. I took a moment to breathe her in, the scent of her acting like a soothing balm to the storm of emotions within me.

The chorus of revving engines brought me back to reality. The time had come. I gave Ava one last lingering look before climbing onto my motorcycle. Her hand found mine, her grip strong and reassuring.

The ride to Night Prowlers' territory was a blur, my mind occupied by thoughts of Ava, the impending battle, and the uncertainty that lay beyond. The clubhouse of the Night Prowlers loomed ahead, a stark reminder of the confrontation that awaited us. I glanced at Ava one more time, her face a mask of steely determination.

The attack happened swiftly, a storm unleashed upon the unsuspecting Night Prowlers. The deafening roars of gunfire and engines had become the symphony of our attack. We were a formidable force, the Boneyard Brotherhood and our allies, a united front against the Night Prowlers. In the dim light of the early morning, the cold steel of our bikes glinted ominously, a silent testament to the storm we were about to unleash.

Our formation, meticulously planned and executed, was a sight to behold. The heavy-duty bikes were in the front lines, their riders armored and ready for the brunt of the attack. Behind them, our sharpshooters were in position, their eyes focused, fingers steady on the triggers. I caught sight of Van Cleef and Sid, their faces grim but determined.

Maddie was there too, her face hidden behind the dark visor of her helmet, her posture rigid with anticipation.

At the core of our formation was the command center. Ted was there, his grizzled face hard as stone, barking orders into his headset. Beside him, Wilson stood tall and resolute, his gaze sweeping over the battlefield with the calculated calm of a seasoned warrior.

Ava and I were somewhere in between, the lines blurring as we danced our deadly dance amidst the chaos. Ava was a force to be reckoned with, her combat training evident in every move she made. She weaved through the battlefield with grace and precision. Her gun fired round after round, each shot precise, each one finding its mark.

I was a tempest, the rage of the storm coursing through my veins. Every punch I threw, every bullet I fired was for the Boneyard Brotherhood, for Ava. I moved through the battlefield with a single-minded focus, my world narrowing down to the fight at hand.

As I took in the field of battle, I also noted the presence of our allies, the third biker club that had joined us in this fight. Their colors were different, their bikes varied, but they fought with the same ferocity, the same determination. Among them, I recognized a few faces, fellow veterans like us who had found a new family in the brotherhood of bikers.

Their leader, a burly man with a grizzled beard and a gnarled scar that twisted down his cheek, was at the forefront. He fought with a brutal efficiency, his large fists smashing into the Night Prowlers with bone-crushing force. His name was Briggs, a former Marine who'd seen more than his share of combat. I'd met him a few times before, and his loyalty to his men was as palpable as his respect for the Boneyard Brotherhood.

Behind him, his second-in-command, a wiry woman named Jazz, was a whirlwind of fury. She was a blur on her nimble sports bike, zipping between opponents, her twin handguns barking in the early morning light. Her shots were precise, each one hitting its mark with deadly accuracy. I could see why she was Briggs' right hand.

Their presence, their solidarity with us, added to the strength of our force. As one, we were a united front against the Night Prowlers. Our numbers, our unity, our sheer determination made us an imposing force. Our bikes roared, our guns blazed, and our war cries echoed in the still morning air, a clear testament to our resolve.

The allied biker gang wasn't just aiding us in this fight; they were fighting for their own reasons, their own past grudges with the Night Prowlers. Their grudges fueled their fury, adding to the intensity of the battle. But at this moment, we were all brothers and sisters on the battlefield, bound by a common enemy and a shared purpose.

At one point, I glanced over my shoulder to see Cole and Dylan, back to back, their faces set in fierce determination. They were a formidable pair, their synergy a testament to their bond. Further away, I caught sight of Chase and Tara, their coordinated attacks causing havoc among the Night Prowlers' ranks.

Despite the chaos around us, I was acutely aware of Ava, her presence like a beacon in the madness. We were connected, not just by our shared past, but by something deeper, something intangible. We moved in sync, our actions mirroring each other's, our hearts beating in rhythm with the drum of war.

In the heat of battle, I couldn't help but marvel at Ava. Her every move was a testament to her training, her resilience. She was a whirlwind of power and grace, a force of nature in her own right. Her presence was a beacon in the chaos, a guiding light that kept me grounded.

Amidst the mayhem, our eyes locked. There was a spark, a connection that transcended the battle around us. Guided by an impulse, I reached out to her, my hand gently caressing her face. Her eyes closed briefly, leaning into my touch.

In the cacophony of the battle, I found myself whispering, "I love you, Ava."

Her eyes flicked open, surprise etching her features. The battle raged on around us, but for a moment, it was just us, lost in our own world amidst the chaos.

"What did you say?" she asked, her voice barely audible above the noise.

"I said, I love you," I repeated, looking into her eyes.

Ava stared at me, the surprise in her eyes melting into something softer, something vulnerable. "Alex," she began, her voice choked with emotion.

But before she could respond, a shout rang out, pulling us back to the grim reality. We had no time for heartfelt confessions. There was a battle to be won.

With a last look at Ava, I charged back into the fray. My heart pounded in my chest, not from the adrenaline of the fight, but from the words I had just spoken. I had confessed my love for Ava amidst a battlefield, not knowing if we would live to see another day.

The battle raged on, a blur of violence and noise. But through it all, Ava was a constant presence by my side. We fought back to back, our movements synchronized as if we were one. Every time I struck down an enemy, I could feel her fighting with me, her presence as real as the battle cries around us.

Finally, after what felt like an eternity, the Night Prowlers began to retreat. We had managed to hold them off, for now. I found Ava amidst the chaos, her eyes meeting mine. We were both battered and bruised, but we were alive. We had survived.

As the dust settled, I walked over to Ava. Her eyes were wide, her breathing heavy. She looked at me, her gaze searching mine.

"Alex," she said, her voice barely a whisper. "You... you meant it? What you said during the fight?"

I reached out, tucking a loose strand of hair behind her ear. "Every word, Ava," I said, looking into her eyes. "I love you."

Ava looked at me, her eyes filling with tears. And then, she was in my arms, her body shaking as she sobbed. I held her, my heart aching for her. We had survived the battle, but the war was far from over. But as long as we were together, I knew we could face anything.

With the smell of smoke and gunpowder still thick in the air, I held Ava close, our hearts beating in sync amidst the chaos. The world around us may have been in shambles, but in that moment, holding Ava in my arms, I felt a sense of peace. Because despite the chaos, despite the danger we were in, one thing was clear to me.

I loved Ava, and I would do anything to protect her. And as I held her in my arms, I made a silent vow to myself. No matter what happened, no matter how dangerous things got, I would keep Ava safe. Because she was more than just my fellow warrior, more than a fellow member of the Boneyard Brotherhood.

She was the woman I loved. And I would go through hell and back for her.

Chapter 18

Ava

As the dust of the battlefield started to settle, the grim reality of the war we'd just waged against the Night Prowlers sank in. I was standing beside Alex, both of us panting from the ferocity of the battle, surrounded by the remnants of the brutal conflict. Fallen brothers, allies, and enemies alike littered the ground, their silent forms a testament to the brutality of the war we had fought.

"Are you okay?" Alex's voice, roughened from shouting orders, cut through the eerie silence.

I looked at him, taking in the hard set of his jaw and the weariness clouding his normally vibrant blue eyes. "I've had better days," I admitted. His hand found mine, giving it a reassuring squeeze.

He offered a weary half-smile. "We all have, Ava." He paused, glancing around the battlefield. "But we held our ground. We defended our own. That's something."

It was a hollow victory, I thought, but I just nodded. The time to mourn and count our losses would come. But for now, we had to gather our strength, regroup and prepare for what was next.

Just as Alex and I were about to turn away, Ted and Wilson joined us. Their faces were etched with exhaustion, their bodies worn from the conflict, but their eyes held a fiery determination.

"We've got a situation," Ted announced, his voice weighed down by fatigue.

"What is it?" Alex asked, his grip on my hand tightening.

Before Ted could respond, Cole stepped forward. The grim set of his jaw spoke volumes. "It's Derek," he said, his voice low and filled with contempt.

The name hit me like a sledgehammer to the chest. Derek. My ex-boyfriend from my military days, the man who'd been stalking me. But to discover he was the puppeteer behind the Night Prowlers' horrific actions was a shock that left me reeling.

"Derek?" Ted echoed, his brow furrowing. "And how do you know this?"

Cole met Ted's gaze evenly. "You don't want to know, Ted."

Silence hung heavy in the air as the others absorbed the revelation. I felt Alex's grip on my hand tighten, a silent promise of protection.

"Derek..." I began, my voice barely above a whisper. "He's an ex from my military days. He's been... he's been stalking me."

I felt Alex stiffen beside me. I'd told him about Derek, about our history. But hearing it confirmed that Derek was behind the Night Prowlers' actions...I knew it would hit him hard. He'd protect me, I knew that.

For a moment, no one said anything. The only sound was the eerie whisper of the wind through the battered landscape.

Finally, Ted broke the silence. "You think this Derek is behind the Night Prowlers?"

"Not think, know," Cole replied, his voice firm. "We had a run-in with him a little while back. He was in the club parking lot, harassing Ava."

Ted shot a glance at me, concern and anger mingling in his gaze. I nodded, confirming Cole's statement.

"Alex and I... we dealt with him," Cole added, a note of satisfaction creeping into his voice. "But it seems like he didn't get the message."

A humorless chuckle slipped from Alex's lips. "He will."

I felt a shiver run down my spine at the ice-cold promise in his voice. I had no doubt that Alex meant every word.

"What do we know about his connection with the Night Prowlers?" Wilson asked, turning his gaze to Cole.

Cole shrugged. "Not much, other than he's been seen with them a few times. But considering what we've just been through, it's clear he's giving them something."

"Or he's using them to get to Ava," Alex interjected, his voice dark.

I squeezed his hand. "We'll deal with him, Alex. Together."

He gave me a grim nod. "Together."

Ted sighed heavily. "Alright. We need to find out more about Derek's involvement with the Night Prowlers. Cole, I want you to dig into this. Ava, Alex, we're going to need your help as well."

"We're in," I said without hesitation, Alex nodding beside me.

"Good," Ted said, his gaze sweeping over all of us. "We've won this battle, but the war is far from over. Let's regroup, tend to our wounded, and prepare for what's next. The Boneyard Brotherhood will not be broken."

With that, he turned and walked away, Wilson following close behind. I looked up at Alex, his face a hard mask, but his eyes soft for me. As we went to follow the others back to our bikes, I knew we were in for a fight. But together, there was nothing we couldn't face.

Derek had made a dangerous move. But he was about to learn just how united the Boneyard Brotherhood could be.

Chapter 19

Alex

The familiarity of the clubhouse, with its ever-present scent of motor oil and worn leather, was a soothing balm after the exhausting face-off with the Night Prowlers. But the comfort was short-lived; Ava looked on edge, her lips pressed together in a tight line.

"Ava?" I placed my beer on the table, feeling a knot of worry tighten in my stomach.

She drew a deep breath, her knuckles white where her hands clenched. "Alex, there's something you need to know."

I frowned, my pulse quickening in apprehension. "What is it?"

"Derek," she began, her voice shaking slightly. "There's more to our history than I've told you."

My heart hammered against my ribs. "Ava, I know he was your ex-boyfriend. You mentioned that."

She shook her head, the pale glow from the overhead lights illuminating her tear-brimmed green eyes. "It's more than that, Alex. He... he overstepped boundaries."

A chill spread through me, icy and brutal. "What are you saying, Ava?"

She hesitated, then let out a ragged breath. "He forced himself on me, Alex. He didn't listen when I said no. That's why I left the military."

A surge of fury washed over me, so intense it nearly blinded me. "That son of a bitch... I'll kill him."

"No, Alex!" Ava's hand shot out, gripping my arm. "That's not what I want."

"What do you mean that's not what you want?" I growled, unable to contain the raw anger in my voice. "He hurt you, Ava!"

"I know," she said, her voice trembling but resolute. "But I don't want you to get hurt because of me."

"He has to pay, Ava," I insisted, images of Derek's destruction blazing in my mind.

"He will, Alex," Ava implored, her grip tightening on my arm. "But not like this. We need to stay united, for each other and for the Brotherhood."

Her words bounced off my red-hot rage. Unable to bear the sight of her tear-streaked face, the revelation of her pain, I jerked away from her grip. "I need to be alone."

Before she could say another word, I turned and stalked out of the room, my boots echoing through the otherwise silent clubhouse. I could feel Ava's gaze on my back, but I didn't turn around.

Chapter 20

Ava

I watched as Alex stormed out of the room, the heavy metal door slamming shut behind him. I could still feel the echo of his anger in the air, a palpable force that made my skin prickle. His reaction was exactly what I'd feared - an all-consuming rage that made him blind to reason. I knew he was fiercely protective, and his reaction to Derek's actions only confirmed it.

I let out a shaky breath, wrapping my arms around myself as if that could hold me together. I felt a chill seeping in, the rawness of my confession still stinging. I had exposed a part of my past that I had hoped to keep buried, and the weight of that reality was crushing.

Suddenly, I felt a soft touch on my shoulder. I looked up to find Dylan standing next to me. Her brown eyes were filled with concern, the harsh clubhouse lights making them glisten. "Hey, Ava," she said softly.

"Hey, Dylan." I tried to offer a small smile, but it felt more like a grimace.

She didn't seem to mind. "Are you okay?"

I shrugged, trying to appear nonchalant. "I will be. I just... I-."

"He really cares about you, Ava," Dylan said, her voice gentle. "His reaction... It was about his anger towards Derek, not disappointment in you."

"I know," I replied, although I wasn't sure if I fully believed it. "It's just... hard."

She nodded sympathetically. "I get it. It's a lot to process. And it's not easy dealing with these guys and their stubbornness. Believe me, I've had my fair share of arguments with Cole."

I chuckled weakly. "I can imagine."

"But remember," she continued, her grip on my shoulder firming, "they may be hard-headed, but they're also loyal. They'll do anything for the people they care about. And Alex... he cares about you, Ava."

Her words warmed me, offering a glimmer of hope amidst the turmoil. Alex was angry, yes, but he was also protective. It wasn't about him being disappointed in me, it was about him wanting to protect me.

"I hope you're right, Dylan," I murmured, finally meeting her gaze.

She squeezed my shoulder and offered me a reassuring smile. "I know I am, Ava. Just give him some time."

I nodded, feeling a little better. With her comforting words and the solidarity of the Boneyard Brotherhood, maybe we could face the storm ahead.

Chapter 21

Alex

My mind was a roiling storm, a tempest of anger and disbelief, as I strode away from the clubhouse. The image of Ava's tear-streaked face haunted me, but the fury boiling in my veins overpowered any sense of rationality.

"Derek," I spat the name out like a curse. The bastard who had hurt Ava, used her... He was the one responsible for the pain in her eyes, the shadows that lurked behind her usually bright, beautiful gaze. The fact that she'd kept this from me, that she'd been carrying this burden alone, only fueled my anger further.

I kicked at a loose rock on the ground, sending it skittering across the asphalt with a sharp crack. The night was cold, but I barely felt it. All I felt was the inferno raging within me, and the need - the need to make Derek pay.

I was aware that I was being irrational, letting my emotions dictate my actions. I knew that Ava wouldn't want me to act this way, that she'd want me to think clearly, to be reasonable. But how could I be reasonable when every fibre of my being was screaming for retribution?

"Alex!" I heard Ava's voice behind me, her plea slicing through the deafening roar of my thoughts. I paused but didn't turn, my fists clenching at my sides.

"Alex, please," Ava implored, her voice closer now. I could hear the tremor in it, the fear. And it cut me deep, deeper than any physical wound could.

"Leave me alone, Ava," I growled, my voice a low rumble of warning. I couldn't face her right now. Not when the image of Derek touching her was etched so vividly in my mind.

"But Alex-"

"I said, leave me alone!" I snapped, spinning around to face her. The hurt in her eyes nearly undid me, but I was too consumed by my rage to let it.

I stalked off into the night, leaving Ava standing there. I knew I was being a jerk, that I was hurting her when she was already in pain. But I just... I couldn't control the anger, the betrayal. The thought of Ava, my Ava, being hurt like that...

As I distanced myself from the clubhouse, I could feel the anger slowly ebbing away, replaced by a hollow emptiness. I knew I had to get a handle on my emotions, that I had to think clearly for Ava's sake, for the Brotherhood's sake. But right now, all I could think about was the pain in Ava's eyes, and the man who had put it there.

Suddenly, my phone buzzed in my pocket, jolting me from my thoughts. It was a text from Van Cleef. "Alex, we need to talk. Clubhouse. Now."

I hesitated, my thumb hovering over the screen. I wasn't ready to face Ava yet, wasn't ready to face the Brotherhood. But if Van Cleef was calling a meeting, it had to be important. With a deep breath, I turned back towards the clubhouse, steeling myself for what was to come.

The walk back to the clubhouse felt like the longest I'd ever taken. Each step was a battle between my anger and my sense of duty. I knew

I was needed, that there were bigger things at stake, but the thought of facing Ava, of seeing the pain I'd caused her... it was almost too much.

As I pushed open the door to the clubhouse, the murmur of voices hit me. The Brotherhood was gathered around the bar, Van Cleef at the center. He glanced at me as I entered, his gaze sharp. He was a womanizer, sure, but he was also one of the most reliable guys I knew.

"Alex," he acknowledged, a hint of relief in his voice. "Good, you're here."

I just grunted in response, taking a seat on the edge of the group. I could feel their eyes on me, a mixture of curiosity and concern. I knew they had heard, or at least sensed, the argument between Ava and me. It was hard to keep secrets in a tight-knit group like this.

"We've got a situation," Van Cleef started, his voice serious. "Something big's going down with the Night Prowlers."

I forced myself to focus on his words, to push aside thoughts of Ava and Derek. I was here for the Brotherhood, for the club. I had to be present, had to be ready to act.

"What's going on?" I asked, my voice rough.

Van Cleef shared a glance with Ted, the leader of our club. Ted was a grizzled veteran, a man of few words but great wisdom. His nod was all the permission Van Cleef needed.

"Derek's made a move," Van Cleef said bluntly. "He's trying to rally the Night Prowlers, make them more aggressive. More dangerous."

A collective murmur went through the group. The Night Prowlers had been a thorn in our side for years, but Derek's involvement changed things. It made it personal. For all of us, but especially for me.

"What's our move?" I asked, clenching my fists. I wanted to do something, anything, to wipe that smug smile off Derek's face.

Ted sighed, rubbing a hand over his face. "We need to be smart about this, Alex," he said, his voice heavy. "Rushing in without a plan isn't the answer."

I knew he was right. I knew we needed a strategy, a plan. But all I could think about was Ava, and the pain Derek had caused her. The pain he was still causing her.

"We'll figure this out," Ted promised, his gaze stern but understanding. "We always do."

After the meeting wrapped up, I stormed out of the clubhouse, my pulse pounding in my ears. The rage and betrayal were like a storm inside me, twisting and turning, threatening to pull me under. I walked aimlessly through the darkened streets, my mind a whirlwind of thoughts and emotions.

Images of Ava, so vibrant and strong, kept flashing through my mind. Mixed with these were flashes of Derek's face, a smug grin playing on his lips. The thought of him, of what he had done to Ava, made my blood boil. I could feel the rage simmering just beneath the surface, a volcano on the brink of eruption.

The more I walked, the more restless I became. The anger wasn't subsiding, it was growing, feeding off my own helplessness. I felt like a caged animal, my instincts screaming at me to act, to retaliate.

Eventually, I found myself back at the clubhouse. The noise, the laughter, the camaraderie - it all seemed a world away.

Without a word, I moved towards my bike. I could feel the gazes on me, even through the windows, questions hanging in the air. But I ignored them. Right now, there was only one thing on my mind - Derek.

I swung my leg over my bike, the familiar feel of the leather seat beneath me a small comfort. The engine roared to life, the sound echoing through the night. I shot one last look towards Ava, her face pale, her eyes wide. Then, with a surge of determination, I kicked off, my bike shooting forward into the night.

Derek was going to pay. I was going to make sure of that.

Ava

I watched as Alex's bike disappeared into the inky blackness of the night. The roar of his engine lingered in the air, a haunting reminder of his departure. A knot of fear twisted in my stomach. I knew where he was going. I knew what he intended to do.

Without wasting another second, I rushed out of the clubhouse, my boots echoing on the gravel. My heart pounded in my chest as I approached my bike. It was a sleek, black beast, a symbol of my independence and strength. Right now, it was my only hope of reaching Alex in time.

I swung my leg over the seat and fired up the engine, its low growl echoing Alex's earlier departure. The familiar vibrations against my palms were a comfort, grounding me as my mind whirred with worry.

I tore off into the night, following the path I knew Alex would have taken. The world blurred past me, the cool night air whipping against my skin. Fear gnawed at me, but I shoved it down. I couldn't afford to be afraid. Not now.

It didn't take long to reach the Night Prowlers' clubhouse. It was a desolate, run-down place that seemed to cower under the weight of its past sins. The windows were boarded up, the doors chained. It was clear that no one had been here since the attack.

Except for one.

Alex was there, standing in the middle of the deserted lot. His tall silhouette was stark against the moonlit backdrop. His fists were clenched at his sides, his entire body radiating tension and anger. He was a ticking time bomb ready to explode.

"Alex!" I called out, my voice echoing in the silent night. He turned around, his blue eyes blazing with an intensity that took my breath away. There was no recognition in his gaze, only raw, unfiltered rage.

"What the hell are you doing here, Ava?" he snapped, his voice a low growl.

"I could ask you the same thing," I retorted, my heart pounding in my chest. "You can't just rush off like that, Alex. You're going to get yourself killed."

His laugh was bitter, devoid of any real humor. "And what? You're going to stop me?" he challenged, his gaze daring me to try.

"Yes," I said firmly, meeting his gaze head-on. "Because I care about you, Alex. And I won't let you throw your life away on a senseless act of revenge."

The tension between us was palpable, a live wire ready to snap. I could see the conflict in Alex's eyes, the war he was fighting within himself. He was at the edge, teetering on the brink of something dangerous. I just hoped I could pull him back before it was too late.

I took a deep breath, steeling myself before slowly approaching him. As I neared, his tension was palpable, like a storm brewing on the horizon. But I didn't let that deter me. I reached out, touching his arm lightly. He stiffened, but didn't move away.

"Alex," I said softly, my heart pounding in my chest. I could feel the heat of his anger, but beneath it, I could also sense his pain, his hurt. And it was that pain I wanted to soothe.

Without waiting for him to respond, I moved closer, wrapping my arms around his rigid body. It was like hugging a statue, but I held on, pressing my body against his. I could feel the rapid beat of his heart against my chest, matching the rhythm of my own.

Slowly, I felt him relax, his rigid posture softening as he melted into my embrace. His arms found their way around me, pulling me closer. I felt his breath hitch, and I tilted my head up to meet his gaze.

His blue eyes were a stormy sea, swirling with a mix of emotions that made my heart ache. I wanted to reassure him, to let him know that he wasn't alone in this. So, I did the only thing I could think of - I kissed him.

It was a soft, lingering kiss, full of comfort and promise. I poured all my feelings into it, hoping he'd understand. When we broke apart, his eyes were softer, his anger dimmed. But I could still see the determination burning in his gaze, a flame that I knew wouldn't be easily extinguished.

"Alex," I whispered, pressing my forehead against his. "Please... let's handle this together. We're stronger as a team."

He didn't respond, but he also didn't pull away. As we stood there, wrapped in each other's arms, I could only hope that my words had reached him, that I'd managed to calm the storm, at least for now.

Chapter 22

Ava

The night was eerily silent as we stood outside the desolate Night Prowler's clubhouse. The air was heavy, thick with tension and lingering anger. Alex stood a few feet away from me, his broad shoulders tense, his fists clenched at his sides. The echo of our heated argument still hung between us, a raw wound that neither of us knew how to heal.

"I'm scared, Ava," he said suddenly, his voice barely more than a whisper. His confession hung in the air, raw and vulnerable. "I'm scared of losing you to him, to his violence. I... I can't bear the thought of it."

His words hit me like a punch to the gut. Alex, the strong, resilient man I had fallen for, was admitting his deepest fears to me. And they revolved around me. It was heartbreaking and humbling all at once.

"Alex," I said, stepping closer to him, "You won't lose me. Not to Derek, not to anyone. I'm not that scared girl anymore. I'm stronger now, and I won't let him hurt me again."

There was silence as he digested my words, his icy blue eyes searching mine for any trace of doubt. But all he would find there was determination and resolve. I had been through too much to let Derek control my life any longer.

Slowly, as if he was scared I would vanish into thin air, Alex reached out and pulled me into his arms. His grip was firm yet gentle, a perfect contradiction that was so uniquely him. His heartbeat was a steady rhythm against my chest, a comforting reminder of his presence.

"I need you, Ava," he murmured into my hair, his voice low and raw with emotion. "I need you more than I've ever needed anyone."

The words, so heartfelt and honest, sent a shiver down my spine. I swallowed hard, my heart pounding in my chest. I had never seen Alex so vulnerable, so open. It was both terrifying and endearing.

"I need you too, Alex," I admitted, my voice trembling slightly. "You... you make me feel safe. Loved."

With those words, the tension between us seemed to ease a little. He pulled back slightly, his hand cupping my cheek as he leaned down to capture my lips in a slow, searing kiss.

His lips moved over mine with a soft desperation, pulling me closer until there was no space left between us. His other hand found its way to my waist, pulling me tightly against his body. I could feel every line of his muscular form, the heat of his skin seeping through the fabric of our clothes.

The kiss deepened, our tongues tangling together in a dance as old as time itself. I clung to him, my fingers digging into the leather of his jacket, needing to feel him, to assure myself that he was real, that this was real.

Our shared vulnerability had ignited a flame between us, a flame that burned brighter and hotter with each passing second. We were two broken souls, finding solace and strength in each other. And right now, in this moment, that was all that mattered.

"I love you, Ava," Alex whispered against my lips, his words sending a jolt of electricity through me. "I love you, and I'll do whatever it takes to keep you safe."

And as I looked into his eyes, those deep blue pools that held so much love and fear, I knew he meant every word. And I also knew that I felt the same way about him.

"I love you too, Alex," I replied, my voice choked with emotion. "And together, we'll face whatever comes our way."

Alex's confession left the air between us charged, thick with emotions too potent to name. His words, laced with a tangible fear of losing me, stung and soothed all at once, stirring a tempest within me. His vulnerability was a siren's call to my own, beckoning me towards him, towards a union that was more than just physical.

His heated gaze found mine, the intensity of his blue eyes making my heart flutter. An unspoken invitation passed between us, a silent command that had me following him towards his sleek, black motorcycle.

His hands, rough yet tender, guided me to bend over the bike's seat. The cool leather pressed against my abdomen as he stood behind me, his strong, muscular body a wall of warmth against my back. His fingers traced the curve of my hips, squeezing lightly, setting off a series of tingles that coursed through my body.

The faint rustle of fabric being unzipped echoed in the quiet night, a stark reminder of the intimacy we were about to share. The cool night air kissed my skin as my jeans were pulled down, leaving me bare to him. A shudder coursed through me, not from the chill, but from the anticipation of his touch.

"Are you okay with this, Ava?" His voice was gruff, laced with desire yet underscored by a genuine concern that warmed my heart.

I nodded, words failing me. His question, so caring amidst our mounting passion, fanned the flames of my desire. I wanted him. More than anything.

A throaty growl vibrated against my back as his hands resumed their exploration, trailing paths of fire across my skin. His fingers teased the sensitive flesh between my thighs, his touch light yet firm. The sensation was electrifying, drawing a soft gasp from my lips.

His fingers danced over me, coaxing, teasing, until I was a quivering mess of need. The world narrowed down to the feel of his fingers on my body, each stroke, each caress sending jolts of pleasure through me.

And then he was there, pressing against me, ready to bridge the gap between us. A gasp tore from my lips as he entered me, filling me in a way that was both overwhelming and utterly satisfying. He stilled, his breath hot against the nape of my neck, waiting for me to adjust to his size.

Alex's rhythm was our unique tempo, a melody composed of our combined desires. Every roll of his hips, every breath he took in time with his movements, created a harmony that resonated deep within me. His hands moved to my hips, fingers digging into my flesh with a bruising intensity that was deliciously painful. His hold anchored me to him, grounding me amidst the swirling sea of pleasure.

"Feel good, Ava?" he breathed, his voice rough with restraint. His words sent a shiver down my spine, the sound echoing in my ears like a sweet serenade.

"Mmm," was all I could manage, my senses overwhelmed by the sensations coursing through me. The edges of my vision blurred as my focus narrowed to the feel of him moving within me.

"That's it, babe," he encouraged, his words punctuated by a particularly deep thrust that left me breathless. "Let me hear you."

His command was a balm to my inhibitions, freeing me to let out the moans and cries that came naturally. Every pleasured gasp, every soft whimper was an ode to the ecstasy he was bestowing upon me.

His grip on my hips tightened as he increased his pace, his movements becoming more erratic. I could feel him tremble against me, his control fraying at the edges as we spiraled together towards our climax.

I gripped the handlebars tighter, my knuckles turning white under the strain. The cool metal under my fingertips was a stark contrast to the heat radiating from our joined bodies. The world outside our bubble ceased to exist as my body moved in tandem with his, our rhythm becoming more frantic.

"Alex!" My voice came out as a strangled cry, the pleasure building within me reaching its peak. His name was a plea, a chant, a prayer spoken in the throes of passion.

"I know, Ava," he responded, his voice strained as he struggled to maintain control. "Hold on, babe. Let's... let's come together."

His words spurred me on, the promise of shared release a tantalizing prospect. I could feel the coil of pleasure within me tighten further, ready to snap at any moment. My body moved instinctively, meeting his thrusts with an urgency that mirrored his own.

The world exploded around me as my climax hit, a wave of pleasure so intense it left me breathless. I screamed his name, the sound echoing around us, a testament to the pleasure he had given me.

His own release followed soon after, a growl of satisfaction rumbling from his chest as he buried his face in my neck. We stayed there, inter-twined and panting, as the waves of pleasure receded, leaving us basking in the afterglow of our shared intimacy.

"Ava," he murmured, his voice soft and filled with a tenderness that sent a warm thrill through me. His fingers traced lazy patterns on my hips, a soothing gesture that grounded me amidst the whirlwind of emotions coursing through me.

I turned my head to look at him, our eyes meeting in the dim light. His gaze was soft, filled with an emotion so raw and pure it took my breath away. "Yes, Alex?"

His lips curled into a small, satisfied smile. "I meant what I said, Ava," he said, his voice barely above a whisper. "I won't let anything happen to you."

His promise, spoken amidst the intimacy of our shared moment, seared itself into my heart. With a soft smile, I reached up to cup his cheek, my thumb tracing the stubble on his jaw. "And I won't let anything happen to you, Alex. We're in this together."

In the quiet solitude of the Night Prowler's clubhouse, we remained entwined in front of his bike, basking in the afterglow of our shared pleasure. Our bodies were entwined like two puzzle pieces fitting perfectly together, and in that moment, I felt an inexplicable sense of belonging.

"Promise?" he asked, the vulnerability in his eyes cutting through the dim lighting.

"I promise," I said, leaning into his touch as he gently brushed a strand of hair away from my face. His touch was softer now, absent of the fiery desire from earlier but filled with a warmth that made my heart flutter.

His fingers traced the curve of my cheek, a soft smile playing on his lips as he looked at me. His gaze was intense, holding a wealth of emotions that left me breathless. The intimacy of the moment, the raw emotion in his gaze, made me feel cherished in a way I had never experienced before.

As his hands continued their exploration, I could feel my body responding to his touch. The sensitivity heightened from our previous encounter, each brush of his fingers sending a new wave of tingles coursing through me.

"Alex," I moaned, my voice coming out as a soft whimper. His touch was intoxicating, a potent mix of tenderness and desire that had my body yearning for more.

"Shh," he murmured, his lips brushing against the sensitive spot behind my ear. The sensation sent a shudder through me, my grip on the bike handlebars tightening.

His movements were unhurried, his fingers tracing a path across my body that left me wanting. The anticipation was maddening, yet the slow build-up was a pleasure in its own right.

His touch became more insistent, his fingers dipping into places that had me gasping for breath. His name slipped from my lips in a breathy moan, the sound echoing in the quiet night.

"Do you trust me, Ava?" His question, laced with a hidden depth of emotion, brought me back from the brink of pleasure.

I nodded, my voice failing me. Trust him? I trusted him more than anyone else. The bond that we had formed, the connection we had shared tonight, had solidified that trust.

His lips found mine in a searing kiss, his tongue exploring my mouth in a dance as old as time. The intensity of the kiss left me breathless, my heart pounding against my ribcage. Alex lifted me and placed me onto the seat of his bike in a delicate balancing act. I wrapped my legs around him, pulling him towards me as he entered me.

And then he was moving within me again, his movements slow and deliberate. The sensation was overwhelming, yet utterly satisfying. His rhythm was a dance of intimacy, each thrust sending waves of pleasure coursing through me.

His grip on my hips tightened as he increased his pace, his movements becoming more erratic. The pleasure was building, a coil of anticipation winding tighter and tighter within me. I held onto him, my fingers digging into his muscular back as I rode the waves of pleasure.

"Alex," I gasped, my body tightening around him as an explosion of pleasure ripped through me. His name was a plea, a chant, a prayer spoken in the throes of passion.

His own release followed soon after, his body tensing against mine as a growl of satisfaction rumbled from his chest. We stayed there, intertwined and panting, as the waves of pleasure receded, leaving us basking in the afterglow of our shared intimacy.

"I love you, Ava," he murmured, his voice soft and filled with a tenderness that made my heart flutter. His fingers traced idle patterns on my back, a soothing touch that grounded me.

I turned to look at him, my eyes meeting his in the dim light. "I love you too, Alex."

Chapter 23

Ava

The sun was just beginning to peek over the horizon as Alex and I pulled into the parking lot of the Boneyard Brotherhood's clubhouse. The events of the previous day were still fresh in my mind, the raw emotions leaving a bitter taste in my mouth. But there was no time to dwell on it. We had a mission to complete.

The clubhouse was already buzzing with activity as we entered, the members of the Brotherhood preparing for the upcoming confrontation. Ted was standing in the center of the room, a map of the city spread out on a table before him. Sid and Wilson were by his side, their faces set in grim determination.

"Good, you're here," Ted said as we approached. His gaze moved from me to Alex, a hint of concern in his eyes. "We were just about to start."

I looked at Alex, taking in his rigid stance and the hard set of his jaw. The anger and hurt from yesterday's revelations were still present, but they were overshadowed by his determination. He gave my hand a reassuring squeeze, a silent promise that we were in this together.

"All right, let's get to it," Alex said, his voice steady. He moved to stand beside Ted, his gaze focused on the map.

Ted cleared his throat, commanding the attention of the room. "We've got a big day ahead of us, folks. Derek and his goons won't know what hit them."

A murmur of agreement swept through the room, the air crackling with a mix of anticipation and determination. I could feel the energy in the room, a tangible manifestation of our collective resolve.

"We've gathered some intel on Derek's whereabouts," Wilson chimed in, pointing to a spot on the map. "He's holed up here, in an old warehouse on the east side."

Van Cleef, who had been quietly observing until now, spoke up. "And we're sure it's him? Not some decoy?"

Wilson nodded, a grim expression on his face. "We're sure. One of our contacts spotted him there yesterday."

I swallowed hard, my heart pounding in my chest. The reality of the situation was starting to sink in. We were really going to do this. We were going to confront Derek.

"I want to be a part of the operation," I declared, my voice ringing out in the silent room.

A heavy silence fell over the room. I could feel everyone's eyes on me, their gazes filled with surprise and concern. But I held my ground, meeting their stares with determination.

Ted was the first to break the silence. "Ava, this isn't a game. It's dangerous."

"I know," I replied, my voice steady. "But this is my fight too."

There was another pause before Ted finally nodded. "Alright. If you're sure, Ava. We need all the help we can get."

A wave of relief washed over me, followed closely by a surge of determination. I was going to be a part of this. I was going to help bring Derek down.

The rest of the meeting was a blur of strategy and planning. Everyone had a role to play, and we all knew the stakes. As the meeting came to a close, Ted stood, his gaze sweeping over each of us.

"Tomorrow, we bring Derek down," he declared, his voice echoing in the silent room.

A chorus of agreement followed his words, the room filling with a renewed sense of determination. I looked over at Alex, his hand still entwined with mine. His blue eyes met mine, filled with a mix of pride and concern.

"We're in this together, Ava," he said, his voice a soft murmur in the quiet room. "We're going to end this once and for all."

I nodded, my heart swelling with a mixture of love and gratitude. "Together," I agreed, squeezing his hand.

As we left the meeting, the weight of the impending confrontation settled heavily on my shoulders. The Brotherhood was united in our goal, but I couldn't help but worry about the dangers we would face. Lives were at stake, and the thought of losing anyone, especially Alex, was almost unbearable.

But I pushed those thoughts aside, focusing instead on the task at hand. We had a job to do, and I was determined to see it through. For myself, for Alex, and for the Boneyard Brotherhood.

The remainder of the day was spent in preparation. Weapons were cleaned and checked, ammunition was gathered, and tactical gear was organized. The air was heavy with anticipation as the members of the Brotherhood moved through the clubhouse, each person focused on their part in the upcoming confrontation.

As night began to fall, Alex and I found ourselves standing alone in the quiet of the parking lot. His eyes were distant, lost in thought, and I knew he was replaying the upcoming confrontation in his head. I slipped my hand into his, intertwining our fingers, and the tension in his frame eased a fraction.

"Let's go to your place," I suggested, nodding to his sleek, black motorcycle parked nearby. "We could both use a break from all this."

He hesitated for a moment, then nodded, giving my hand a reassuring squeeze. "Sounds like a plan."

The ride to his apartment was a silent one, the purring of our motorcycles the only sound breaking the quiet of the night. Once we arrived, we shed our jackets and boots, the familiar actions grounding us in the face of the storm brewing on the horizon.

Alex wrapped his arms around me from behind, pulling me back against his chest. His breath was warm against my neck as he whispered, "We'll get through this, Ava. Together."

I turned in his arms, gazing up into his piercing blue eyes. There was a fierceness in his gaze, a promise that gave me strength. "I won't let anything happen to you, Alex," I said, my voice steady despite the turmoil swirling within me. "I promise."

We held each other in the dim light of his apartment, our bodies a comforting warmth against the chill of uncertainty. As I rested my head on his chest, listening to the steady thump of his heart, I knew we were ready to face whatever came our way. Together, we would confront Derek and put an end to his reign of terror, whatever the cost.

Chapter 24

Alex

The day of the showdown had finally come, the early morning sun casting long shadows over the Boneyard Brotherhood's clubhouse. I could feel the tension in the air, like a tightly wound spring ready to snap. I scanned the room, my gaze falling on each member of the Brotherhood. The faces of my brothers were hard, their expressions grim. Despite the danger we were about to face, there was a sense of solidarity that held us together.

Ted stood at the front of the room, his grizzled face etched with determination. "Alright, we all know why we're here," he began, his voice ringing out in the silence. "Derek's been a thorn in our side for far too long, and it's time we dealt with him once and for all."

Sid nodded in agreement. "Ain't gonna be easy, but it's gotta be done." He looked towards Maddie, who gave him a supportive squeeze on his arm.

I felt Ava's hand slip into mine, her touch a reassuring warmth against the anxiety gnawing at my gut. Turning to look at her, I found her emerald eyes fixed on me, a silent vow of support shining in their depths.

"We're with you, Alex," she said softly. Her words were a balm, soothing the tumultuous emotions roiling within me.

Ted continued outlining the plan, his words echoing in the hushed room. "We need to be smart about this. We can't afford any unnecessary risks. We strike hard and fast, and then we get the hell out of there."

I stepped forward, all eyes turning towards me. "I'll lead the charge," I offered. My voice was steady, betraying none of the apprehension I felt. "I won't let that bastard get away this time."

Ted nodded approvingly. "Good. We'll need all the firepower we can get."

A murmur of assent rose from the crowd. I could see the resolve in their eyes, the unwavering determination to bring Derek to justice.

The rest of the meeting was a blur of strategy and logistics. Plans were made, roles assigned, and contingencies discussed. Each member of the Brotherhood knew what they had to do. The calm before the storm was ending, and we were ready to face the tempest.

When the meeting finally adjourned, Ava and I found ourselves alone in the clubhouse. She looked at me, her green eyes reflecting the turmoil I felt inside.

"We can do this, Alex," she said, her voice barely above a whisper. "We've faced worse."

I nodded, drawing her closer. "I know. I just..." I paused, struggling to put my feelings into words. "I just don't want to lose you, Ava."

She reached up, her fingers gently tracing the contours of my face. "And you won't, Alex. I promise."

We roared out of the clubhouse, our motorcycles cutting through the early morning silence. The adrenaline began to surge through my veins, a familiar rush that came with every operation. We were finally heading to confront Derek.

When we arrived at the rendezvous point, an isolated strip of land on the outskirts of the town, I was relieved to see a sizeable group of the

Brotherhood already assembled. Beyond the familiar faces of Ted, Wilson, Van Cleef, Sid, and Chase, there were other club members present too - some I knew well, others I had only exchanged a few words with. But today, we were united by one common purpose.

"Okay, here's the plan," I said, stepping forward. "Ted, Sid, Van Cleef - you're on diversion at the front. Chase, you've got our six. Wilson, you're with Ava and me."

Nods of understanding echoed around the group. As my gaze locked with Ava's, her face was set in a mask of determination.

"We'll take him down, Alex," she said, her voice steady and resolute.

With the plan laid out, we advanced towards Derek's hideout, a dilapidated warehouse in the industrial district. As we approached the looming structure, my heart pounded in my chest. This was our moment of reckoning.

We dismounted our bikes a safe distance away, and moved into position with practiced stealth. Ted, Sid, and Van Cleef melted into the shadows, heading for the warehouse's front entrance, while Chase took up position at our rear.

"All right, let's do this," I murmured, leading Ava and Wilson through the murky darkness.

Near the entrance, I signaled Ava and Wilson to hold their positions. Peering around the corner, I saw two guards, remnants of the Night Prowlers, lounging by the door.

In a swift motion, I launched myself at the guards. My fist connected with the first one, and he crumpled to the ground. The second one barely had time to react before he was taken down.

Footsteps approached, and I spun around, ready for another fight. But it was Ava and Wilson, their faces grim in the entrance light.

"Nice work," Ava said, a small smile playing on her lips.

There was no time to reply, as the sound of gunfire echoed from the front of the warehouse - the signal that Ted's diversion had begun.

With one last glance at Ava and Wilson, I kicked open the warehouse door, leading the way into the lion's den. The battle with Derek and what was left of the Night Prowlers was about to begin.

The inside of the warehouse was dim, the only light came from a couple of bare bulbs hanging from the ceiling. My senses heightened, alert to every sound, every possible movement. The smell of oil and decay filled my nostrils. I glanced back at Ava and Wilson, seeing the same focused readiness in their eyes. We had entered the enemy's lair, but we were prepared.

As we pressed forward, my mind raced. I was caught between the pressing urgency of the mission and the protective instinct I felt for Ava. I knew she was more than capable - we had trained together, fought together - but my heart clenched at the thought of her in danger. I shook off the feeling; I had to focus.

We moved cautiously, our boots silent on the concrete floor. I felt a tingle on the back of my neck and spun around just in time to see a figure lunging at us from the shadows. I acted instinctively, landing a solid punch to his gut before Wilson took him down with a swift kick.

"Thanks," I said, nodding at Wilson.

"No problem," he replied, his focus already back on our surroundings.

We pressed forward, taking down a few more Night Prowler stragglers who tried to stop us. Each takedown was efficient and quick, our combined skills and experience evident.

Suddenly, a group of four goons appeared, blocking our path. They were bigger than the others, likely Derek's personal guards. I glanced at Ava and Wilson, determination set in their eyes.

"Let's do this," I said.

We launched ourselves into the fight. Ava went for the one on the left, her movements fluid and swift. She was a whirlwind of strength and precision, a sight that would have left me in awe if we weren't in such a dangerous situation.

Wilson and I teamed up against the other three. We moved in tandem, our combined force overpowering them. It was brutal and messy, but we were winning. And then, just as the last goon fell, a chilling voice echoed through the warehouse.

"Well, well, well. If it isn't my dear Ava and her new playmates."

Derek stepped out of the shadows, a smug grin on his face. The final confrontation was upon us.

"Should've known you'd bring a welcoming party, Derek," Ava retorted, her voice steady. Despite the situation, I couldn't help but feel a surge of pride for her courage.

"Always the tough one, aren't you?" Derek sneered, his eyes raking over Ava in a way that made my blood boil. "Remember when you used to be mine?"

"Never was, never will be," Ava shot back. Her gaze met mine briefly, offering me a silent assurance. I nodded, ready to stand by her side.

"Well, let's see about that," Derek growled, lunging at Ava.

I instinctively moved to intercept him, but Ava held out her hand to stop me. "I've got this, Alex," she said firmly. I hesitated, my protective instincts screaming at me. But I saw the determination in her eyes, and I knew I had to let her face him.

As Ava and Derek squared off, Wilson and I held back, ready to jump in at the first sign of trouble. I watched as Ava dodged Derek's first swing, countering with a swift punch to his midsection. I could see the surprise on his face as he staggered back.

The fight was brutal and intense. Derek was strong, but Ava was fast and agile, using her military training to her advantage. I watched, my heart pounding, as she landed blow after blow, her face set in a grim line of determination.

Suddenly, Derek managed to grab Ava's arm, twisting it behind her. A gasp of pain escaped her lips and I tensed, ready to jump in. But before I could move, Ava spun, breaking his hold and slamming her elbow into his face. Derek stumbled back, a hand to his nose.

"That's for what you did to me," Ava spat, her green eyes blazing with anger.

Before Derek could recover, Ava lunged, landing a final blow that sent him sprawling to the ground, unconscious.

As the dust settled, I rushed to Ava's side, my heart pounding with relief and admiration. She had faced her demon and come out victorious. As I pulled her into a tight hug, I couldn't help but feel a surge of pride.

"You did good, Ava," I whispered into her hair. She nodded, her breath shaky against my chest. The fight was over, and we had won.

Together, we turned to Wilson, who was looking at us with a mixture of respect and admiration. "Let's tie him up and get him back to the clubhouse. The Brotherhood will decide his fate."

The remnants of the Night Prowlers had been defeated, their leader captured. As we walked out of the warehouse, Ava's hand in mine, I felt a profound sense of relief. We had faced the enemy and come out on top. Today, the Boneyard Brotherhood stood victorious.

Chapter 25

Ava

The celebration was wild and filled with laughter, with club members and their loved ones filling the clubhouse. Cindy had outdone herself with the food, tables filled with hearty dishes and snacks that were quickly being devoured. Everyone was in a joyous mood, and the air was thick with camaraderie and relief.

Ted was holding court at the head of the bar, his grizzled face creased into a rare smile as he regaled a group with tales of the club's early days. "Back then, we were just a bunch of kids with bikes and a dream," he said, his voice filled with nostalgia. "Look at us now. We've come a long way."

Chase Miller and Tara were engaged in a friendly arm-wrestling contest nearby, their faces strained with effort as a crowd of onlookers cheered them on. "Don't you dare let me win, Miller!" Tara shouted, her determined expression eliciting laughs from the crowd.

Elsewhere, Van Cleef was flirting with a group of women, his charm and wit on full display. Nearby was Maddie, who was deep in conversation with Dylan and Sid.

Seeing them, I walked over, Alex in tow. Sid was massaging his lower back, a grimace on his face. "Back giving you trouble again, Sid?" I asked, concerned.

He waved me off. "Just the old war wounds acting up. Nothing a few beers can't fix."

Dylan rolled her eyes at him. "Or you could let me take a look at it later," she offered. "You know, like a responsible adult."

Sid laughed. "Where's the fun in that?"

Just then, Cole sauntered over, a grin on his face. "Did I hear someone challenging my woman's medical advice?" he asked, wrapping an arm around Dylan.

Sid raised his hands in surrender. "I wouldn't dare, Cole. I value my life too much."

The group erupted in laughter, and the conversation flowed naturally from there, covering everything from the latest motorcycle upgrades to plans for the next club ride.

Alex and I drifted around the room, chatting with different members, sharing jokes and stories. The atmosphere was festive, filled with a warmth and connection that was uniquely Boneyard Brotherhood.

As the night wore on, Chase and Tara took control of the jukebox, filling the room with a mix of classic rock and country tunes. Couples and friends paired off on the makeshift dance floor, their movements a blend of coordinated steps and drunken sways.

Van Cleef tried to pull me into a dance, but Alex was quick to intervene. "Sorry, Van Cleef, this one's mine." He led me to the dance floor, his arms wrapping around me as we swayed to the music.

"We did it, Ava," he murmured in my ear. "We faced hell and came out the other side."

I smiled up at him. "We did, didn't we? Together."

As we moved with the rhythm of the music, lost in each other's eyes, I felt a profound sense of contentment. This was where I was meant to be. With Alex. With the Boneyard Brotherhood.

After what felt like an eternity, Alex led me to a quieter corner, his hands gripping mine. His blue eyes were serious, the festive noise around us fading into a distant hum.

"Ava," he began, his voice barely above a whisper. "There's something I've been meaning to ask you."

And then he was down on one knee, a small velvet box in his hand, a diamond ring glinting in the dim light. The question hung in the air, a moment of pure anticipation as the noise of the party receded into a blur.

"Ava," he said again, his gaze locked onto mine. "I love you. More than I ever thought I could love anyone. You're strong, resilient, brave, and so damn beautiful. You've stood by me, by us, through some real tough times. You've become a part of this brotherhood, a part of me. I don't want to face another day without knowing you're mine, truly mine. Ava, will you marry me?"

Time seemed to stand still as I stared at Alex, his proposal ringing in my ears. A cacophony of emotions surged within me, surprise, joy, love, all converging into an overwhelming tide. Around us, the room had fallen silent, all eyes on us, but all I could focus on was Alex, the sincerity in his eyes, the love.

"Yes," I said, my voice a choked whisper. "Yes, Alex, I will."

A cheer erupted around us, loud and jubilant, but all I could hear was the rapid beat of my heart and Alex's relieved laugh. He slipped the ring onto my finger, a perfect fit, before pulling me into his arms and capturing my lips in a passionate kiss.

Chapter 26

Ava | Three Months Later

The rays of the morning sun streamed through the window, bathing the room in a soft, golden light. I lay in the comfort of the sheets, my body still tingling from the events of the previous night. Alex, now my fiancé, slept soundly beside me, his arm draped protectively around my waist. His chest rose and fell rhythmically against my back, the steady beat of his heart a comforting rhythm in the silence.

Staring at the engagement ring on my finger, a beautiful round diamond set in a simple silver band, a surge of joy filled my heart. It was more than just a ring. It was a symbol of our love, our commitment, our future. I gently ran my fingers over the cool metal, the diamond catching the sunlight and scattering it across the room.

I turned to look at Alex, his face peaceful in sleep. The sight of him filled me with an overwhelming sense of love. I traced my fingers lightly down his stubbled cheek, my heart swelling with affection. This was the man I was going to marry, the man I wanted to spend the rest of my life with.

"Good morning, beautiful," Alex murmured, his eyes fluttering open. He pulled me closer, his warm lips finding mine in a tender morning kiss. "How's my future wife doing?"

"Better than ever," I replied, nestling into his embrace. His strong arms tightened around me, his warmth seeping into my skin.

As the morning turned into afternoon, we found ourselves at the clubhouse, the Brotherhood buzzing with excitement over our upcoming wedding. Cindy, the cook at the clubhouse and a woman with an inexplicable knack for organization, had taken it upon herself to plan the entire event. She bustled around with a clipboard in hand, barking orders at the members and making sure everything was going as per her plan.

Maddie was conscripted into helping Cindy with the decorations, while Tara was given the task of coordinating security for the big day, and Dylan, Cole's better half, was assigned the responsibility of managing the guest list and invitations.

I sat in the center of it all, a flurry of fabric swatches, flower samples, and catering menus swirling around me. Alex, who had been trying to hide a smile at my overwhelmed expression, was caught by Cindy and given the task of choosing the menu for the reception.

"Okay, so we have three potential caterers," Cindy announced, spreading out several folders in front of Alex. "I need you to look at their menus and tell me what you think."

Alex nodded, flipping through the first folder. "I don't know, Cindy. I think whatever we choose will be great."

Cindy rolled her eyes. "Just pick something, Alex. We don't have all day."

Meanwhile, Maddie approached me with an armful of fabric swatches. "Ava, we need to decide on the colors. What do you think about this combination?" She held out a swatch of deep green fabric alongside a piece of soft gold.

"It's beautiful, Maddie," I said, taking the fabrics from her. "I think it would look lovely."

"Great," Maddie beamed, crossing something off a list she held. "Now, let's talk about flowers."

Tara, who had been busy coordinating with a few of the Brotherhood's members, walked over to us. "Security is covered," she said, giving me a thumbs up. "We'll make sure no unwanted guests crash your special day."

"Thanks, Tara," I said gratefully. "I know I can count on you."

"Alright, Ava," Dylan chimed in, joining our little huddle with a notepad in hand. "I've got the guest list here. I just need you to double-check and make sure we didn't miss anyone."

The hours flew by as we navigated through the labyrinth of wedding planning. Despite the chaos and the overwhelming amount of decisions to be made, I couldn't help but feel a surge of joy. We were planning our wedding, a day that signified the start of our new life together. And we were doing it surrounded by people who loved and cared for us. It was more than I could've ever wished for.

As night fell, the clubhouse was abuzz with energy, laughter, and camaraderie. But for all the joy that filled the air, there was a part of me that yearned for a moment of tranquility, a brief reprieve from the wedding planning chaos.

Just as I was contemplating an escape, Alex caught my eye from across the room, his gaze soft and inviting. He nodded subtly towards the door, and I followed his lead, sliding out of the clubhouse unnoticed.

"Follow me," he murmured, his voice barely audible over the sounds of the wind rustling through the trees. He hopped onto his bike and I followed suit, the purr of our engines intertwining as we rode off into the darkness.

We rode in silence, the night cool and crisp around us. The path was familiar, and my heart fluttered in anticipation as Alex guided us towards the clearing where we had first made love under the stars. The memory of that night, of the raw passion and tender love we had shared, sent a shiver down my spine.

As we parked our bikes and dismounted, the clearing was bathed in soft moonlight, casting long shadows and illuminating the wildflowers that bloomed in the grass. Alex took my hand, leading me to the center of the clearing, our boots crunching softly on the forest floor.

"Ava," he murmured, pulling me close. His breath was warm against my neck, causing goosebumps to rise on my skin. "I want to make a new memory here, one that intertwines with the past but points us towards our future."

I tilted my head up to meet his gaze, my heart pounding in my chest. "Alex," I whispered, my voice barely audible over the rustling of the trees.

He silenced me with a kiss, his lips soft and insistent against mine. His hands roamed my body, igniting a trail of fire wherever they touched. As our bodies entwined, the world fell away, leaving nothing but Alex and the intoxicating connection between us.

With each kiss, each touch, Alex was staking a claim, and I was willingly surrendering, lost in the sensation of him. I felt the heat of his body against mine, the rough fabric of his clothes against my skin. My hands traced over the muscles of his back, feeling the strength that lay beneath.

His lips moved from my mouth, down my neck, and along my collarbone. His touch was a mixture of gentleness and insistent desire that left me breathless. "Alex," I breathed, my voice shaky, "you make me feel... I can't even describe it."

A low chuckle vibrated through him. "I hope it's good, Ava," he murmured against my skin, his hands skimming down my sides to rest at my hips. "Because you... you make me feel alive. Like everything before this was just existing."

His words, so raw and sincere, hit me right in the chest. This was the Alex I loved – vulnerable, passionate, real. I wrapped my arms around him, pulling him closer, wanting to erase any distance that might have existed between us.

"Alex," I said, my voice barely above a whisper, "I love you. More than I ever thought possible."

His eyes, so blue and intense under the moonlight, met mine. "And I love you, Ava," he replied, his voice thick with emotion. "With everything I am, and everything I have."

His confession, so heartfelt and earnest, sent a wave of emotion crashing over me. He loved me, and I loved him, and in that moment, it felt like nothing else in the world mattered.

He kissed me again, his mouth moving over mine with a fervor that matched my own. I felt his hand move to the hem of my shirt, his fingers tracing circles on my skin, leaving a trail of goosebumps in their wake. The sensation was intoxicating, and I found myself craving more.

"Is this okay?" he asked, his voice hoarse with desire, but still making sure I was comfortable.

"Yes," I breathed, my heart pounding in my chest. His hand slipped under my shirt, his touch setting my skin on fire. He traced the curve of my waist, his fingers gentle but confident as he explored. I arched into his touch, a low moan escaping my lips. His touch was like a live wire, sending jolts of electricity straight to my core.

His fingers traced up my ribcage, his touch light as a feather, and yet it had my body thrumming with anticipation. My breath hitched when his hand cupped my breast, his thumb grazing over the sensitive peak. A gasp escaped my lips, my back arching as a wave of pleasure washed over me. His name fell from my lips like a prayer, my hands clutching at his shoulders.

"God, Ava," he groaned, his forehead resting against mine. "You're so beautiful, so responsive. I can't get enough of you."

I could feel my face heating up at his words, but the look in his eyes, the raw desire and adoration I found there, made me feel beautiful and wanted in a way I'd never felt before. His lips found mine again, stealing my breath away as his hand continued its maddening exploration.

Our bodies moved together, a dance as old as time, yet fresh and exhilarating because it was us. Alex's kisses grew more demanding, his body pressing me into the soft grass, but I welcomed his weight, welcomed the feel of him against me.

He moved to unbutton my jeans, his gaze never leaving mine, always seeking consent. I nodded, my fingers moving to his belt, mirroring his actions. There was a sense of urgency, a need to feel skin on skin, but it was mixed with a tenderness that had me teetering on the edge.

As our clothes were shed, the cool night air was a stark contrast to the heat that radiated between us. Alex's gaze roamed over me, his eyes dark with desire. "You are so beautiful," he whispered reverently. His fingers traced over my curves, leaving a trail of goosebumps in their wake. I shivered, not from the cold, but from the intensity of his gaze, the intimacy of his touch.

Alex moved over me, his body shielding me from the cool air. Our bodies aligned perfectly, his hard length pressing against my core. He took his time, his hands and mouth exploring every inch of me, leaving no part of me untouched. I writhed beneath him, my body aching for more.

And then he was pushing into me, filling me. I gasped at the sensation, my hands clutching at his back. He stilled, giving me time to adjust before he began to move. His strokes were slow and deliberate, each one sending a wave of pleasure coursing through me. His name fell from my lips in a breathless whisper, my body moving in rhythm with his.

Our eyes locked, and in that moment, everything else fell away. There was only us, only this. His pace quickened, his movements becoming more urgent, more desperate. I matched his rhythm, my body meeting his thrust for thrust. The pleasure was building, a pressure coiling in my lower belly, ready to snap.

"Alex," I gasped, my body trembling. "I'm... I'm..."

"I know, love," he murmured, his lips finding mine in a searing kiss. "Let go, Ava. I've got you."

His words were my undoing. The coil in my belly snapped, and I cried out, my body convulsing as waves of pleasure crashed over me. Alex followed soon after, his body tensing before he collapsed on top of me, his breath ragged.

We lay there, a tangle of limbs, our bodies still joined. The night was silent, save for our heavy breathing and the occasional hoot of an owl. The moment was perfect, and as I lay there in Alex's arms, his heart beating in sync with mine, I realized that this was more than just physical intimacy. It was an emotional connection, a moment of complete vulnerability and trust.

His fingers traced lazy patterns on my skin, his touch gentle and comforting. His breath tickled my ear as he whispered, "I love you, Ava."

"I love you too, Alex," I murmured back, snuggling deeper into his embrace. His words weren't just an echo of what I'd said earlier. They were a promise, a vow, a pledge of his love and commitment.

The emotional intensity of the moment left me feeling raw and exposed, but in the best possible way. I felt seen, understood, loved. Alex's arms around me felt like home, a safe harbor in the storm.

As our breathing evened out and our bodies cooled, Alex pulled the blanket we'd brought closer, wrapping it around us. The night was quiet, the stars above twinkling like a million tiny diamonds. The world seemed to hold its breath, as if giving us this moment of peace and tranquility.

"I could stay here with you forever," Alex murmured, his lips brushing against my forehead.

"In this clearing?" I teased, my heart fluttering at the sincerity in his voice.

He chuckled, the sound rumbling through his chest. "Anywhere, as long as I'm with you."

His words, so simple yet so profound, brought tears to my eyes. I looked up at him, seeing my own emotions reflected back at me. "Promise?" I asked, needing to hear him say it.

His gaze held mine, steady and unwavering. "I promise, Ava."

And I believed him. In the quiet of the night, under the watchful eyes of the stars, I believed in us. Despite all the odds, despite everything that stood in our way, I believed in our love.

Chapter 27

Alex

The Brotherhood clubhouse was a hive of activity as I stood there, clad in a suit that felt a bit too tight and formal for my liking. The grungy, hard-living space had been transformed into a wedding venue, complete with white drapes, strings of twinkling fairy lights, and a makeshift aisle leading to a rustic arch at the center. The transformation was surreal, but it felt right - it was us.

My heart pounded heavily against my ribcage, a steady drum of anticipation and nerves. I watched the Brotherhood members milling about, adjusting decorations, checking security perimeters, and doing last-minute tasks. Ted, with his tough exterior softened by the occasion, was issuing orders, making sure everything was in place. Wilson, his usual second-in-command, was at his side, nodding along.

Van Cleef was teasing Sid about his clean, pressed shirt and polished boots, while Cole was deep in discussion with Chase about something I couldn't hear. Dylan and Tara were helping Cindy set the long tables with pristine tablecloths, gleaming silverware, and fresh flowers.

The atmosphere was thick with camaraderie and a familial warmth that permeated every corner of the clubhouse. This was our family, our Brotherhood, and I couldn't imagine a better group to stand beside us as Ava and I pledged ourselves to each other.

The low hum of a motorcycle engine cut through the sounds of laughter and chatter, drawing everyone's attention to the entrance. My heart leaped in my chest as Ava rode in, her long, dark hair billowing out from under her helmet. She was dressed in a white leather jacket and matching pants, the outfit hugging her curves and enhancing her beauty.

As she dismounted her bike and removed her helmet, I caught my breath at the sight of her. Her green eyes sparkled with excitement and love, her lips curled up in a radiant smile. She looked beautiful, captivating, and utterly mine.

The clubhouse fell silent as she walked down the aisle towards me, her every step confident and graceful. Her eyes locked onto mine, and I could see a world of love and promise in them. My heart pounded even harder as she stood in front of me, her hand reaching out to take mine.

"Alex," she began, her voice steady, her gaze unwavering. "You've shown me that love isn't just about romance and sweet words. It's about standing by each other, supporting each other, and fighting for each other. You've been my rock, my protector, and my partner. You've made me believe in love again, and for that, I can't thank you enough."

Her words struck a chord deep within me, resonating with my own feelings for her. I squeezed her hand gently, my gaze never leaving hers.

"Ava," I responded, my voice thick with emotion. "You've shown me that love isn't about perfection or having it all together. It's about being real, being vulnerable, and accepting each other for who we are. You've accepted me, flaws and all, and loved me in ways I never thought possible. You've given me a reason to live, to fight, and to love."

Tears welled up in her eyes, but she blinked them away quickly, her smile never fading. Ted stepped forward then, his gaze solemn as he began the ceremony. The Brotherhood watched us, their eyes gleaming with happiness and pride.

As we exchanged vows and rings, the air seemed to crackle with intensity and emotion. Our voices echoed through the silent clubhouse, our promises to each other ringing clear and true. As we sealed our vows with a kiss, the Brotherhood erupted in cheers, their applause thunderous in the enclosed space.

passed in a blur of laughter, dancing, and heartfelt toasts. The Brotherhood members took turns sharing stories of their experiences with us, some funny, some touching, and some downright embarrassing. Each tale was a testament to the bond we all shared, the family we had formed, and the love we were celebrating.

Van Cleef and Ted took turns roasting me in their speeches, much to the amusement of the crowd, while Sid and Cole shared heartfelt stories of Ava's strength and loyalty. Maddie and Dylan, both beaming with pride, spoke of the sisterhood they had found in Ava and how her resilience had inspired them. Chase and Tara recounted the moment they had first met us and how they knew, even then, that we were meant to be together.

As the night wore on, the music grew louder, and the Brotherhood members took to the dance floor, their movements uninhibited and joyful. Ava and I danced together, our bodies pressed close, her laughter like music in my ears. The love that radiated between us seemed to infuse the air, lending an almost magical quality to the celebration.

Eventually, as the night drew to a close, the Brotherhood members began to disperse, leaving Ava and I standing hand in hand in the now-empty clubhouse. We were exhausted but elated, our hearts full of love and gratitude for the incredible day we had just shared.

With a tender smile, Ava led me to our room, where the soft glow of candles and the scent of rose petals greeted us. The intimacy of the moment washed over us, our eyes meeting in a look of unspoken understanding and desire.

As we undressed each other, our touches were slow and deliberate, a dance of passion and love that spoke volumes. We explored each other's bodies, as if for the first time, savoring every sensation, every caress, and every kiss.

Our lovemaking was slow and tender, a testament to the love that bound us together. Our bodies moved as one, our breaths mingling, our hearts beating in unison. As we reached our peak, the world around us seemed to fall away, leaving only the two of us, our love, and our commitment to each other.

Exhausted, we collapsed into each other's arms, our bodies slick with sweat and trembling with the aftershocks of passion. As we lay there, entwined and sated, I knew that this was just the beginning of our life together - a life filled with love, loyalty, and the unbreakable bond we shared with eachother.

Chapter 28

Ava

The early morning light filtered through the curtains of our hotel room, casting a soft, golden glow over everything it touched. We were far away from the clubhouse, tucked into a secluded resort for our honeymoon. I woke to the comforting warmth of Alex's body curled around mine, his strong arms holding me close. I couldn't help but smile, my heart swelling with love for this man.

The past few weeks had been a whirlwind of emotions, a mix of fear, anticipation, joy, and finally, absolute contentment. We were married. Alex was my husband. And I was his wife. The reality of it was still sinking in, but every time I looked at the gold band on my finger or felt the press of his lips against mine, it became more real.

As I lay there in his arms, I found myself thinking about the journey that had brought us here. The battles we'd fought, the obstacles we'd overcome, the bond we'd forged. It hadn't been easy, but then again, nothing worthwhile ever was.

Alex stirred behind me, his breath tickling the nape of my neck. He pressed a kiss to my shoulder, his voice rough with sleep. "Morning, Mrs. Malone."

I turned in his arms to face him, my fingers tracing the line of his jaw. "Morning, Mr. Malone."

He grinned at me, his blue eyes sparkling with love and happiness. "How does it feel to be on our honeymoon?"

"I could get used to this," I said with a smile, snuggling closer to him. "It's nice to be away from everything, just the two of us."

He brushed a strand of hair away from my face, his gaze tender. "I think we both needed this. Time to decompress, to just... be."

I nodded, my heart aching at the love in his eyes. "I love you, Alex."

"I love you too, Ava."

We spent the morning lounging in bed, talking about everything and nothing. It was during these quiet moments that Alex opened up about his past, telling me stories of his time in the military, the missions he'd been on, the friends he'd lost. It was a side of him I'd rarely seen, a side he'd kept hidden beneath a layer of protection and secrecy.

But now, here on our honeymoon, he let down his guard. He shared his fears, his regrets, his hopes for the future. And I listened, my heart aching for the pain he'd endured, my love for him deepening with each word he spoke.

After our lazy morning in bed, we decided to venture out. Our honeymoon resort sat nestled on the coastline, and the wide stretch of beach was inviting. We grabbed our beach gear, and hand in hand, we made our way to the private beach that the resort offered. The sand was warm beneath our feet, the waves lapping gently at the shore.

Alex flashed me a mischievous grin. "Race you to the water!"

With that, he took off running, his laughter echoing around us. I gave chase, my own laughter joining his. We plunged into the clear, cool water, our bodies colliding. He wrapped his arms around me, pulling me close. We kissed, the taste of saltwater on our lips.

Next, we decided to try windsurfing. We took a quick lesson from the instructors at the beachside shack, and soon we were out on the water, trying our best to balance on the boards.

"You're a natural at this, babe," Alex called out, his voice carrying over the waves.

I looked over at him, just in time to see him lose his balance and fall into the water with a splash. I couldn't help but laugh, even as I tried to keep my balance. "Spoke too soon, Mr. Malone!"

His head popped out of the water, and he spluttered, shaking his head to clear the water from his eyes. "That was on purpose. I just wanted to show you what not to do."

We spent the afternoon exploring the local town on rented bicycles. We pedaled through the narrow, cobblestone streets, past colorful houses and bustling marketplaces. Alex insisted on buying me a wide-brimmed straw hat from a street vendor, placing it on my head with a flourish.

"There, now you look like a true tourist," he teased, snapping a picture of me with his phone.

I struck a pose, tipping the hat at a jaunty angle. "Does this mean I get to buy you a matching one?"

He chuckled, shaking his head. "I think I'll pass."

That evening, as the sun began to set, we found a quiet spot on the beach. We spread out a blanket and sat down, a picnic basket between us. We feasted on fresh fruits, cheese, and a bottle of champagne, the sound of the waves providing a perfect backdrop.

As the sky turned pink and orange, Alex reached out, taking my hand in his. "This is perfect, Ava. Just you, me, and the ocean."

I leaned against him, my heart full. "It's everything I ever dreamed of, Alex. I love you."

As night fell, we made our way back to our hotel room, our bodies close, our hearts full of love and happiness.

Underneath the soft glow of the room's ambient lighting, Alex's hands found their way to the small of my back, pulling me closer until I could feel his breath fan across my face. His gaze was intense, a mirror to the simmering desire I felt coursing through my veins. When his lips finally claimed mine, a low whimper escaped me, the sound swallowed by the intoxicating rhythm of our kiss.

He moved slowly, deliberately, his hands beginning to explore the landscape of my body. Each brush of his fingers against my skin left a trail of heat in its wake. His touch was like electric sparks, jolting my senses and leaving me wanting more.

"God, you're beautiful," he murmured against my lips before his fingers started to unbutton my sundress. The fabric slipped from my shoulders, pooling at my feet and leaving me in my lacy undergarments. His gaze was searing, drinking in the sight of me as though I was the most precious thing he'd ever seen.

With a gentle push, he guided me towards the bed. I perched on the edge, watching as he carefully rid himself of his own clothes. His movements were fluid, confident, each one tantalizingly slow as if he was putting on a show just for me.

Once he was as bare as I was, he pulled me onto his lap. His hands roamed freely, each touch a brand that seared my flesh. He was everywhere, and I reveled in the sensation, my body reacting to his every touch.

His fingers found the clasp of my bra, skillfully unhooking it. I felt the cool air against my bare chest, making me shiver. But then his hands were there, warm and comforting, cupping me gently. He took a nipple into his mouth, suckling gently. The sensation sent a jolt of pleasure coursing through my body, a gasp escaping my lips.

His hand snaked down my body, slipping into my panties. His touch was like a live wire, causing me to jerk in surprise. His fingers were relentless, delving into my wetness, his actions causing a rush of pleasure that had my head spinning.

"Alex," I gasped, my body responding eagerly to his touch. He didn't say anything, just kept his gaze locked on mine, his eyes dark with desire.

He moved his fingers away, leaving me panting and wanting. But before I could protest, he was pushing my panties down, exposing me completely to his gaze. His eyes held a gleam that made my heart hammer in my chest.

He leaned down, his lips teasing the sensitive area between my thighs. His tongue was a sweet torment, exploring every inch of me, each stroke driving me closer to the edge. My hands gripped the sheets beneath me, my back arching off the bed as pleasure coursed through my veins.

When my climax hit, it was like a tidal wave, washing over me and leaving me shaking. Alex didn't stop until I was spent, my body limp and sated.

But we weren't done, not by a long shot. Alex moved up my body, capturing my lips in a searing kiss. His own desire was evident, his erection pressing against my thigh. My hand moved to stroke him, but he gently swatted it away, a playful smile on his lips.

"We have all night, love," he said, his voice rough with desire.

We moved together, exploring each other's bodies with a newfound curiosity. He took me from behind, his movements slow and deliberate.

The new angle brought a different kind of pleasure, one that had me biting my lip to stop myself from crying out.

Taking a deep breath, I pushed myself up, using Alex as my support, positioning myself over him. I could feel him hard beneath me, his size and warmth making my mouth water with anticipation. Guiding him with my hand, I eased him into me, an audible gasp leaving my lips at the delicious sensation. Every nerve ending in my body sparked to life as I began to move, my hips rolling in a rhythm that was as old as time itself.

Alex's eyes never left mine, the intensity of his gaze making my heart flutter. His strong hands were on my hips, guiding and steadying me as I rode him. He sat up, his back against the headboard, allowing me to lean into him. His mouth found mine, our kisses becoming more passionate as our rhythm increased.

I could feel my body responding to his, a coil of heat winding tighter and tighter within me. My breath hitched as a wave of pleasure washed over me, causing my grip on Alex to tighten. His hands moved from my hips to my breasts, his thumbs brushing over my sensitive peaks, causing me to cry out.

The room was filled with the sound of our mingled moans, the rustle of sheets, and the erotic symphony of our bodies coming together. I could feel my climax approaching, a tidal wave ready to crash over me. Alex seemed to sense this, his movements becoming more purposeful, driving me closer and closer to the edge.

And then I was there, my climax hitting me with the force of a freight train. I cried out, my body convulsing as waves of pleasure washed over me. My inner muscles clenched around Alex, pulling him even deeper inside me.

Alex's grip on me tightened, his body tensing beneath me. With a low growl, he reached his own climax, his release filling me. We rode out our pleasure together, our bodies moving in a slow, languid rhythm.

Exhausted, we collapsed onto the bed, our bodies a tangled mess of limbs. Alex pulled me close to him, his arms wrapping around me protectively. I could feel his heartbeat against my back, a steady rhythm that soothed my frazzled nerves. I closed my eyes, the events of the day catching up with me.

The silence was only broken by our heavy breathing, gradually slowing down as we basked in the afterglow of our lovemaking. I turned my head, pressing a soft kiss to Alex's chest, earning a contented hum from him.

Alex's fingers traced lazy patterns on my back, his touch light and soothing. "We should do this more often," I whispered, my voice hoarse from our earlier activities.

He chuckled, the sound rumbling in his chest. "I couldn't agree more, love."

As I drifted off to sleep, wrapped in Alex's arms, I knew that I had found my home. With him, I was safe, loved, and cherished. I belonged with him, just as he belonged with me. And I wouldn't trade that feeling for anything in the world.

Chapter 29

Ava

We were back from our honeymoon. Back to where it all began. The sound of familiar engines growling, the smell of gasoline and leather, the sight of the Boneyard Brotherhood's clubhouse - it all washed over me like a wave of nostalgia, despite our absence being only a few days.

Ava was clutching my arm, her fingers digging into the leather of my jacket. I glanced at her, catching her brilliant green eyes looking around, taking in the sight. The corners of her mouth curled up in a small, contented smile, and I felt a surge of warmth in my chest. It was a silent affirmation of our commitment, not only to each other but also to the Brotherhood.

A few heads turned as we strolled towards the entrance of the clubhouse. Van Cleef was the first to spot us, a wide grin spreading across his face. "Well, look who it is!" he hollered, raising his beer in our direction.

The rest of the crew followed suit, raising their drinks, the chorus of welcoming cheers echoing around the yard. I tightened my grip on Ava's hand, leading her through the crowd of familiar faces. Despite the recent trials we'd faced, the unity within the Brotherhood was palpable.

As we made our way through the crowd, I noticed Ted leaning against the bar, a knowing smirk on his face. "How was the honeymoon?" he asked, his gruff voice filled with amusement.

Ava blushed, but her gaze remained steady. "Fantastic, thanks for asking," she replied, her voice laced with a hint of defiance that made me chuckle.

"Well, you two sure look... refreshed," Wilson chimed in, his eyes twinkling with mischief. Laughter rippled through the room, but it was warm, devoid of any malice. This was our family, and we were home.

We spent the evening reminiscing about the past, discussing our future, and reaffirming our commitment to the Brotherhood. We shared stories from our honeymoon, intentionally leaving out certain details which resulted in more laughter and teasing.

Ava and I found ourselves alone later, sitting on the roof of the clubhouse, staring at the stars. The noise from the party below was muffled, creating a serene bubble around us. Ava leaned into me, her body warmth seeping through my shirt, and I wrapped an arm around her.

Looking down at Ava, I traced a finger down her cheek, a gesture that had become second nature to me. She turned her head to plant a soft kiss on my palm, her eyes filled with affection.

"We did good, didn't we?" she said softly, her gaze returning to the stars.

"We did," I agreed, pressing a kiss to the top of her head. I felt her sigh contentedly against me, her body relaxing even more.

And as we sat there, under the blanket of the night sky, I couldn't help but feel a surge of peace. We'd faced trials and tribulations, but we'd come out stronger on the other side. We'd chosen each other, chosen this life, and I had no doubt that we were ready to face whatever came our way.

The party was still going strong when we finally decided to join the others. The music was loud, the laughter louder, and the sense of camaraderie was tangible. Ava's hand slipped into mine as we descended the stairs, her fingers squeezing gently. I glanced at her, her green eyes sparkling with life and love.

"Yeah, we did good," I muttered to myself, allowing myself to be pulled into the crowd.

The night wore on, and the laughter and camaraderie never waned. We danced, we drank, and we reveled in the knowledge that our family was reunited and stronger than ever. As the hours ticked by, the celebration began to wind down. One by one, our friends and brothers started to say their goodbyes, leaving Ava and me standing in the now-empty clubhouse.

"We really are home, aren't we?" Ava murmured, her eyes scanning the room as if seeing it for the first time. I nodded, wrapping an arm around her waist and pulling her close.

"We are, and we're going to make it even better," I promised. "Together, we can help the Brotherhood thrive."

Ava looked up at me, her green eyes shimmering with determination. "I know we can," she agreed, her voice filled with conviction. "We've been through hell and back, and we've come out stronger for it."

As we stood there, surrounded by the remnants of our celebration, I couldn't help but feel a renewed sense of purpose. The Brotherhood had been tested, but we'd come out on top, and I knew that together, we could face any challenge that came our way.

And so, as the first light of dawn began to filter through the windows, Ava and I turned to face our future. Hand in hand, we walked into the rising sun, knowing that we had each other, and the Boneyard Brotherhood, to lean on.

Our journey was far from over, and we were ready to face it together. And with love, loyalty, and unwavering determination, we would continue to forge our path forward, stronger than ever before.

Printed in Great Britain
by Amazon